PENGUIN  S0-AAA-346

UNDER A MONSOON CLOUD

H. R. F. Keating was the crime books reviewer for *The Times* (London) for fifteen years. His first novel about Inspector Ghote, *The Perfect Murder*, won the Gold Dagger of the Crime Writers Association and an Edgar Allan Poe Special Award. Having been chairman of the Crime Writers Association and of the Society of Authors, he was recently elected president of the Detection Club.

Under a Monsoon Cloud

H. R. F. KEATING

PENGUIN BOOKS

PENGUIN BOOKS

Viking Penguin Inc., 40 West 23rd Street,
New York, New York 10010, U.S.A.
Penguin Books Ltd, 27 Wrights Lane, London W8 5TZ
(Publishing & Editorial) and Harmondsworth,
Middlesex, England (Distribution & Warehouse)
Penguin Books Australia Ltd, Ringwood,
Victoria, Australia
Penguin Books Canada Limited, 2801 John Street,
Markham, Ontario, Canada L3R 1B4
Penguin Books (N.Z.) Ltd, 182–190 Wairau Road,
Auckland 10, New Zealand

First published in the United States of America by
Viking Penguin Inc. 1986
Published in Penguin Books 1987

Copyright © H. R. F. Keating, 1986
All rights reserved

LIBRARY OF CONGRESS CATALOGING IN PUBLICATION DATA
Keating, H. R. F. (Henry Reymond Fitzwalter), 1926–
Under a monsoon cloud.
I. Title.
PR6061.E26U53 1987   823'.914   86-30665
ISBN 0 14 00.9209 9

Printed in the United States of America by
Offset Paperback Mfrs., Inc., Dallas, Pennsylvania
Set in Baskerville

Under a Monsoon Cloud

1

Inspector Ghote had been awaiting the memo from the Commissioner for a week or more. He knew, too, what it would say almost to the exact words. Yet when the stiff white envelope was put in front of him he felt such a thud of plummeting dismay that it might have been entirely unexpected.

Bombay's tingling pre-monsoon heat, hardly relieved by the fan squeaking away in the corner of his office, struck at him suddenly, as if until this moment it had not existed. Automatically he reached down to the bottom drawer of his desk for the towel he kept there and mopped at the heavy bulbs of perspiration that had sprung up all over his face and neck.

It needed a strong effort of will to pick up the envelope, sweatily stained from the fingers of the peon who had brought it, and tear it open.

The words he read were as heavily ominous as he had anticipated. And all arising, he thought, from one foul prank fate has played on me.

From the Commissioner of Police, Bombay
To: Inspector G. V. Ghote

I have considered certain events alleged to have occurred at Vigatpore PS on the night of June 24/25 last year and I must request a full account of your part therein. I require to have the aforesaid account before me by 0900 hours on Monday, June 4.

He felt sick. Sick as if he had been struck down by food poisoning.

Inspector Ghote's temporary transfer to the police station at Vigatpore, miles distant from Bombay, had been abrupt. He had been summoned one morning by the Assistant Commissioner, Crime Branch, and told that owing to an unprecedented number of officers being unavailable to replace the man in charge at Vigatpore, who had fallen ill, he was being given the posting.

'I am sure you are not having anything too important on your plate itself, Inspector. Pass on whatever has to be dealt with immediately. Anything else can be allowed to wait.'

'Yes, sir.'

On the veranda outside the Assistant Commissioner's office Ghote had stood prey to contradictory feelings. A sudden posting to an unknown area: it would bring all his capabilities to the fore. But, on the other hand, was not his work here in Bombay being rated altogether low? If each and every case before him was something that could be disposed off to someone else at a moment's notice or even left untouched for weeks, then what sort of a report would he get next year on his Confidential Record?

And Vigatpore, it was a bloody backwood only.

He was the sole passenger to alight at the station late that evening and at first there seemed to be no one to meet him, though he had sent a message stating the time of his arrival. For a quarter of an hour and more he paced the deserted platform, soon beginning to fume with bad temper. But just within the time-limit he had set before taking action he heard a vehicle approaching in the stillness of the hot night and a few minutes later a police jeep drew up outside.

He decided not to take its constable driver to task for his lateness and merely watched him in stony silence as he gathered up his luggage and put it in the back of the vehicle. However, as they made their way towards the little hill station he thought it best to chat with the fellow in order to find out what he could about his new responsibility.

He did not discover a great deal, chiefly only such facts about the small town as he had already picked up for himself in the course of the hectic afternoon in which he had sorted out his work-load, explained the sudden move to his wife – Protima had flared into one of her come-and-gone rages – and got together what he would need for an indefinite stay away.

But he did learn from the driver one thing that added to his unease. It seemed the officer he was replacing, Inspector Khan, had arranged for him to stay not at one of the town's hotels but at a private house as a paying-guest.

'It is the residence of Shri Shivram Patel, Inspector. Very, very influential.'

'Oh, yes? What is he then?'

'Now nothing at all, Inspector. But before-before he was chairman of the Zilla Parishad, could say what was to happen in whole damn district.'

'And he is that no more?'

'Achcha, Inspector. You see, he was owning only damn creamery in area and everybody-everybody was having to bring milk to him only.'

'But then?'

'Then they were starting up dairy cooperative, and nobody-nobody was any more selling him milk at price he only was fixing. Inspector, that man is most poor now, and, Inspector . . .'

'Yes?'

'He is damned angry all the time also.'

Ghote sat in silence then, contemplating not without some anger of his own how little bodily comfort he was likely to have during his stay in this place. One of the facts he had found out in his hasty research of the afternoon had been that the word Vigatpore was said to come from the Sanskrit for 'Town of Difficulties'. At the time he had thought what a piece of useless information that was. Now he was not so sure.

Shivram Patel's house when they arrived at it did nothing to alter his feeling. It appeared to be deserted and the driver, after waiting outside the gates for some ten minutes occasionally hooting the horn, was constrained to turn the vehicle until its headlights illuminated an overgrown and neglected compound. Ghote saw a fat bandicoot scuttle rat-like away. There was a gap in the mud wall next to the locked gates, and through it they managed one after another to squeeze.

Even at the massive house door the driver had to tap and tap with the dangling chain with which the place would be padlocked when empty. And it was not until he had thumped hard at the thick timbers that at last a dim light appeared in the window above.

It was followed by the sound of the heavy wooden door-bar being lifted and the door itself was finally opened an inch or two by an ancient servant, grimy and unshaved, holding a dim hurricane lamp, its glass almost totally obscured by soot.

But at least the fellow acknowledged that a paying-guest was expected, though not with any graciousness. In silence then he led Ghote through the house. By the orangey light of the lamp Ghote made out that the rooms they passed on their way to the wide wooden staircase leading to the upper floor were unnaturally bare. No doubt they had once been well furnished. Here and there patches on the walls were visible where hangings or pictures must once have been, and at one point there was even, high up, a distinct round area where in bygone days a large clock must have sonorously ticked out the prosperous hours. But now all was denuded, echoing and starkly uninviting.

Upstairs they trailed along a lengthy corridor and at the far end the old servant ushered Ghote into a small room. Its furnishings seemed to be only an earthen chatti for water in one corner and, looking as if it had been flung down with contempt, a bulging straw mattress.

'This is for you,' the old man muttered.

And then, showing much more shuffling speed than he had done hitherto, he turned and vanished into the darkness.

By the faint light coming through the room's sole window Ghote undressed and lay down on the bulky mattress. At once he felt a dozen different sharp pricks from the straw inside. But, exhausted with all that had happened to him during the course of the day, it did not take him long despite the parching heat to fall into a heavy sleep. The last thought he was conscious of was that next day the new task he had been plunged into would no doubt test his capabilities severely.

And next morning, arriving at the police station good and early, he found that he had, if anything, underestimated what would be required of him.

To begin with, he found waiting to greet him in the small stone building's entrance hall, standing idiotically smiling, an old acquaintance from Bombay. Or, more correctly, an old adversary. Lumpen and lazy, Sergeant Desai had for a short time come under him at Crime Branch, almost certainly after not a little cunning manoeuvring by whatever department had previously been saddled with him. In the end, thanks to an adroit move of his own, he had succeeded in getting the fellow off his neck, but he had hoped never to have to see him again.

And now, at the very start of his difficult enough

assignment here, there was Desai, grinning at him all over his big face, pleased as a dog thumping two tails.

'Very good place, Vigatpore, Inspector,' the fellow began at once, as if continuing some previous conversation. 'Damn good posting. You will like. Oh, yes, sir, stay here as long as you can stop them knowing where you are. Damn fine place. Damn good lake, you know.'

'Lake?' Ghote shot out in fury, feeling the last thing he wanted was a description from this fool of the town's famed Lake Helena. 'What are you talking about?'

'Oh, everybody is knowing the lake here, Inspector. Vigatpore and Lake Helena. Two always go together.'

And on to his smudgy nosed face Desai planked a look of comic-book superiority, the man of experience teaching the novice.

'You remember what a damn fine champion I am in swimming,' he added abruptly.

Ghote did not remember. He doubted if he had ever known. But Sergeant Desai – how had the idiot managed to retain his stripes all this time? – began at once to provide details. At unstoppable length.

'Oh, yes, Ghoteji, many bloody rupees I am winning at bets from that lake. You want to make a bet I cannot cross it, there and back, in two hours only? Five bucks? Ten?'

'That will do, Sergeant.'

He was not going to have the fellow taking familiarities on the strength of the few days they had once worked together, if having Desai sitting on one's head could be called working with him.

Ruffled with irritation he took possession of the office vacated by the suddenly ill Inspector Khan – had Desai's persistent cocksure uselessness driven Khan to a break-down? – and discovered in the course of the morning that in fact the whole station had been run with a lack of efficiency that made Desai's cheerful clumsiness seem almost normal.

He found the office itself monumentally untidy. Softly

flaking files were heaped on every available surface, most of them thick with dust. From the ceiling there actually still hung the remains of a flapping punkah, surely dating from when the station had been built, in the British days, while prominent on the desk was a big brass inkpot, doubtless from the same era, unpolished and bone-dry. The Station House Diary, which he had sent for as soon as he had cleared enough of the desk to work at, did not contain a single entry for the whole past week.

In the days and weeks that followed, more and more of Inspector Khan's errors and omissions came to light. The Bad Character Roll proved to have had no additions made to it for two years. The Muddamal Room, when some time in his second week he got round to inspecting its items of lost property and articles retained as evidence, had no inventory of its contents. Inspector Khan's own Case Diary, that most sacrosanct of volumes, had had more than one page inexpertly ripped out.

As heinous, in a page-numbered book of First Information Reports all three top copies concerning a recent incident were missing and the final fourth copy, which could not be removed without leaving an obvious gap, was so faint as to be almost undecipherable. Attaching a note stating that further action might be required to the pallid blue carbon copy, Ghote saw, with his sense of dismay by then almost dulled, that the incident reported was an attack by goondas on the chairman of the dairy cooperative which had put his temporary landlord out of business. No doubt Shivram Patel had been in collusion with Inspector Khan to thwart an investigation which might show who had been behind the assault.

No doubt, too, the reason he himself had been given such an uncomfortable billet in place of a room at one of the hotels was that Khan was doing the former extortionist owner of the creamery another favour.

For the tenth or eleventh time Ghote wondered whether it

was worth making a fuss and getting himself a new quarter. The straw mattress it was his lot to spend his nights on still contrived to prick him each time he turned over.

But surely his posting must come to an end before much longer.

Certainly there was nothing to be done by complaining to Shivram Patel himself. He had tried that on the first occasion he had met him, several days after his arrival.

He had come upon him unexpectedly as, stomach gurgling from a wretched wayside-stall meal of lukewarm greasy parathas and poor over-stewed tea with buffalo milk, he had been making his way last thing at night to his bare room at the far end of the big old denuded house.

Shivram Patel was carrying a lamp, the sole form of lighting in the house to which electricity was no longer supplied. Seeing his guest, he had held the lantern high and, thrusting a big, bull-like head forward, had peered at him with ferocious dislike.

'Good evening. It is Mr Patel?'

'You. Why for do you have to be in my house?'

'Well, Inspector Khan was arranging that I should be your paying-guest.'

'Paying-guest. Paying-guest. And I have had true guests in this house by the hundred. Musicians I have had for entertaining. Dancing girls also. And now what do I have? A police inspector from Bombay only. Thrust into my middle.'

'Well, but for that you are well paid. And while we are talking the matter, the mattress you are giving me is not at all good.'

'Good-tood. You are lucky to be getting what you are.'

And the big bear of a man had turned and marched away into the darkness.

Ghote saw him only two or three times more during the whole course of his stay. Clearly the former Zilla Parishad chairman had no very high sense of the obligations of the host of a paying-guest. He simply kept out of the way, nursing his grievances like a bear with a fine store of honey suddenly snatched from him. On each occasion they met it was plain that Shivram Patel had somehow focused on this visitor in his house much of the feelings of resentment he had been letting gather like rumbling monsoon clouds over all the time since the rich livelihood he had considered himself entitled to had been brought to an end.

At first Ghote had felt some sympathy for him. His vanished prosperity had been perhaps no more than he deserved after years of living in luxury on what he had extorted from peasants owning only a single cow or a couple of buffaloes. Yet no doubt he had been brought up from childhood to expect as of right the good things the world had to offer, and to have had all this inherited ease swept from underneath him must have been a devastating blow. However, since he had done nothing to come to terms with his changed circumstances, after the second of their meetings, which had been as thunder-charged as the first, Ghote had simply made as little use as he could of the expensive and impoverished accommodation that had been wished on him – doubtless in doing so only adding to his landlord's dislike.

But he had enough worries, as the weeks went by, in battling against the tumbledown neglect and general indiscipline at the station while the heat building up to the monsoon had grown more and more oppressive. Vigatpore as a hill station had a reputation for being delightfully cool in summer. But now it was simply stinkingly hot. Even to think became difficult, and patches of prickly heat, maddeningly itchy on neck and shoulders, made keeping an even temper almost impossible.

The very crows pecking at carrion in Shivram Patel's neglected compound were covered with the reddish dry dust that was everywhere, desiccating tongue and throat, tormenting nostrils. Once in the road on his way to work Ghote saw a bullock that had collapsed from sheer heat between the shafts of its crude country cart. And up and down the little town bands of boys roamed chanting *God, oh God, send us rain, God, oh God, send us grain.*

Even when, at last, clouds began to mass over the surrounding hills they brought no more than an occasional single sigh of breeze to rattle the hard dried leaves of the trees and once or twice short periods of fine drizzle that did nothing to lessen the heat and discomfort. Sergeant Desai, that idiot, took to proclaiming each tinglingly hot day 'The galloping of a horse, the mind of a woman, whether the monsoon will be good or bad, even the gods cannot be predicting.'

Then one afternoon of electric stiflingness, under an ominous hanging mauvish pall of cloud, the clerk from the station's Writers Room came in to Ghote with a message. The station was to be subjected, next day, to an Inspection. Nor was that all. Of all the senior officers who might have had this duty, Vigatpore PS was to be visited by Additional Deputy Inspector-General of Police Keikar. Tiger Kelkar.

Tiger Kelkar was another old Bombay acquaintance of Ghote's, but of a very different sort from Desai. Even when Ghote had worked with him he had had a formidable reputation for drive and efficiency. But – and this made his forthcoming Inspection all the more potentially embarrassing – it had been Ghote's task at that time to suspect Tiger, together with the handful of other picked officers in a cell which had been specially recruited to combat Bombay's powerful black-monkey bosses, of corruptly selling information. Tiger, of course, had proved not to be the rotten apple in the basket, but it had been a duty to view him for all of that period as capable of that betrayal.

However, besides this embarrassment, Tiger Kelkar had a reputation now as an implacable hunter-down of the inefficient with a zeal that showed itself in outbursts of anger feared throughout the force. His Inspection was bound to bring to light omissions and inefficiencies still remaining in the station, and blame for them would descend on the officer in charge, however short the time that he had occupied his seat. Scorching and fearful blame.

2

When early next morning Additional Deputy Inspector-General of Police Kelkar arrived at the station, tall, broad-shouldered, keen-eyed and blade-faced, neat moustache showing only a hint of grey, all Ghote's anxieties rapidly proved justified. Except one. Not by the least flicker of an eyelid did Tiger Kelkar show he harboured resentment over what it had once been Ghote's duty to suspect him of.

'Ah, Inspector,' he said, as Ghote in his best, seldom-worn, rather too tight regular uniform gave him his smartest salute, 'we have been colleagues in the past, have we not?'

'Oh, yes, Kelkar Sahib.'

Ghote had been unable to think of anything more to reply. The already oppressive heat of the day brought sweat prickling to his forehead.

'I will add one thing only, Ghote, while no one else is nearby, so we know where we are standing from the word go.'

'Yes, A.D.I.G.?'

'The fact that we once worked together will make no difference to the manner in which I shall conduct my Inspection. Understood?'

'Yes, A.D.I.G.'

Ghote looked up at him with something akin to awe.

Such a sense of duty. What other senior officer would be able to cut away so completely all pettiness? There were some, he knew, who would have been ready to treat an Inspection with a lenient eye on account of shared experiences in the past. And more, he guessed, would flame with resentment at having once been regarded by his junior with suspicion, and would seize gleefully on a chance to make life hell.

But Tiger Kelkar, upright and strict, had at once shown himself above either attitude.

His Inspection, however, was still a nerve-wracking business, despite the furious preparations Ghote had ordered the day before – the scrubbing, the whitewashing, the tucking away of awkward objects, the polishing.

For a little at the start he was simply all admiration for the way Tiger Kelkar missed not the smallest detail. The torn-out pages from Inspector Khan's Case Diary were snapped up as if by a gecko flicking out its tongue at a passing fly. The long absence of entries in the Bad Character Roll received a single fierce jotting in red ballpoint in Tiger's notebook, and Ghote knew that for years to come no such slackness would be repeated. Wooden chair L4 was found to be missing, something which neither Ghote nor anyone else had noticed. And Sergeant Desai, that fool, came in for a truly terrible pulling-up for having a broken lace in his right boot, something Ghote felt he had really asked for since he himself had not only pointed it out but had also taken the precaution of finding the fellow a task, investigating a minor theft at one of the hotels, that ought to have kept him out of Tiger's way.

But all too soon Tiger's fiery attacks began to search out weaknesses of his own. Even down to the most trivial.

'Inspector, what is this inkpot?'

Ghote looked down at the desk he had ceded to the A.D.I.G. He had long before cleared it of all Inspector Khan's clutter and now it had been polished till it glowed.

The brass inkpot, which had been there when he had taken over, was still in what was presumably its correct place, though shining now more than it appeared to have done for years. So why was Tiger asking about it?

'Inkpot, A.D.I.G. Sahib?'

'Yes, man, inkpot. Inkpot. What the hell did you think I was asking about?'

Outside, a sudden pre-monsoon windstorm had got up. Two or three doors in the building had smacked back against the walls before anybody could shut them. Somewhere on the other side of the road a sheet of corrugated iron had been half-torn from its moorings and was banging and booming like a minor outbreak of gunfire.

Ghote felt as if much such a racketing blast had struck at him.

'The inkpot is a cent per cent correct issue, A.D.I.G. Sahib,' he lied hastily. 'I am already checking up myself.'

'And if it is a proper issue, Inspector, why is it minus any sort of ink? What use do you think is an inkpot minus ink?'

'None, sir. None.'

'Then get it filled, man. Get it filled.'

Quickly Ghote stepped out to look for his peon, whose task presumably it ought to have been to keep the inkpot full. But he scarcely blamed the man – his name was Shinde – for his failure. The fellow was one of the very few things in Vigatpore he felt inclined to put in the credit column. For some reason right from his very first day in the station Shinde, his face lit in splay-toothed smiles, had fixed on him a dog-like admiration. At whatever hour he needed anything the fellow was there, saluting left-handedly and with widespread fingers, ready to get it for him. All that he lacked, and Ghote felt guilty even for recognising this, was any spark of assertiveness. Almost as soon as he had first met him some odd words his father had been fond of repeating, a bit of English poetry, had come into his mind, 'Lords without anger or honour, Who dare not carry their swords', and they came again almost every time he saw the fellow. Poor Shinde would never be asked to carry any sort of sword, but even if he were it was certain he would not dare.

But in the meanwhile, thank goodness, he was quick to get hold of ink and fill the wretched object that had aroused Tiger's wrath.

And as the days of the Inspection went by Tiger's sharp eye spotted more and more deficiencies, and with blasting anger he pointed them out. Soon there was a new air of bustle in the station which he himself, despite all he had achieved, had not wholly managed to instil. The constables looked smarter, the naiks issued orders with more snap, the whole place buzzed. Tiger's temper might be scalding but it certainly produced results. More, Ghote realised, than all his own efforts ever could have done.

Then, as the last day but one of the visit came towards its end and Ghote was beginning to allow himself a glimpse of how pleasant it would be when Tiger was no longer sitting on his head, the first mighty rainstorm of the monsoon burst down on to them. It brought to an end the tingling tension – half caused by the electric heat, half by Tiger's electric rages – that had grown and grown in the station.

It also caused all the lights instantly to go out.

Tiger's voice rose like the crack of a thunderbolt above the sudden mad tom-tomming of the rain on the station roof.

'Emergency generator. Get it going. Get it going.'

With a jolt of pleasure Ghote recalled that, not a week earlier, he had thought to acquaint himself with the emergency lighting arrangements. He set off at once himself for the small annexe where the generator was housed and with his own hands started it up.

It worked. The lights of the building flickered once or twice and then came fully on.

Ghote went back in, secretly patting himself on the back that for this once he had under Tiger's ferocious eye got something altogether right. And Tiger himself was there, standing in the entrance hall.

'Good man,' he said.

Ghote felt a wave of pure warmth spread through him.

But at that precise moment the main door crashed wide open and into the gleamingly polished entrance hall there came staggering Sergeant Desai. Rainwater cascaded off him on to the floor like torrents down a mountainside, and he wore a face-splitting grin as if there had been nothing so delightful since Nataraja danced the world into existence.

'Get that man out of here,' Tiger Kelkar roared.

Desai ought to have turned and fled. Any reasonable individual encountering such a bolt of anger would have done so. But Desai was not a reasonable individual.

'Yes, sir, Mr Kelkar, sir,' he said. 'What man is that, please, sir?'

'You, you idiot,' Ghote shouted, knowing however that his exasperation was more like one of the gusts of wind hurling rain at the station's windows than the lightning of Tiger's anger. 'It is you, you bewakoof. You are making one hell of a mess in here. Get out. Go round and come in somewhere where you won't spoil the whole place.'

'Oh, but, Inspectorji, I am wet only, nothing to mind.'

Ghote froze with rage.

'Inspectorji? Inspectorji? How dare you speak to me in such familiarities. Report to me tomorrow morning and get away off to your quarter before I have you put in the lock-up.'

'I am going, Inspector. I am going. No need to lose the ballyrag.'

Mercifully, before Tiger could say anything more, the fellow did actually reopen the main door and go out into the night, raising both arms to the tumbling rain and giving a yell of ridiculous joy.

As the rest of the long evening wore on, with Tiger showing no signs of slackening in his various inquiries,

Ghote gave permission one by one for all the personnel in the station, which except for a sentry outside was not manned at night, to go to their beds. Tiger next day would no doubt be bustling round everywhere and everybody had better be at their most alert. Besides, now that the monsoon had begun, the men would be anxious to get back to their lines to make sure no wild rain was swirling in through an unprotected window or penetrating a heat-cracked roof.

At last he found himself left only with the dog-devoted Shinde, splay-toothed in smiles and whenever the least occasion arose splay-fingered too in his parody of a salute.

So when yet another roar came from within Inspector Khan's transformed office demanding a certain First Information Reports book Ghote hurried into the Records Room himself. It did not take him more than two or three minutes to locate what Tiger wanted. It was, he saw, the book containing that last feeble copy of the report on the attack on the dairy cooperative chairman, with clipped to it, thank goodness, his own memo recommending further inquiries. He went quickly back to give it to Shinde to take in to Tiger, stickler that he was for the correct way of doing things, had not been pleased when earlier in the evening he had himself brought him a document he had wanted.

'Inspector,' that incisive bark had come, 'have some self-respect. You are not a bloody peon. Don't behave like one.'

But Shinde, the bloody peon, was no longer sitting on his bench outside the office.

Suppressing a flicker of annoyance, Ghote set off to look for him. Faithful though he was, he must after all from time to time have to answer a call of nature.

However, he could find him nowhere. As he hastened back, it just occurred to him to open the door of the Mud-damal Room in case the fellow had gone in there for some reason.

He had not. But in a corner, sitting on an upturned

21

vegetable walla's basket, an idiot grin beginning at once to spread all over his face, was Sergeant Desai.

Ghote could not restrain himself from yelling at the idiot.

'Sergeant. What the hell are you doing here?'

'Oh, this is where I am always hanging my jacket when it is getting wet, Inspector. There is plenty hangers here. Look.'

'I thought I told you to go back to your quarter. And Shinde, have you seen him anywhere?'

'Oh, yes, Inspector, I have seen.'

That and no more.

'Where is he? Where is he, you fool? I am urgently wanting.'

'Oh, I was just only sending to get me a cigarette, Inspector. I am out of stock.'

Ghote felt a bomb of outrage blow up in his head.

'You – You what?' he shouted.

Patiently Desai repeated word for word what he had said before.

Ghote found nothing that he could summon to his lips could at all convey what he was feeling. For several moments he stood regarding the still grinning Desai in blank silence.

'That will be one more thing I will see you about in the morning, Sergeant,' he blasted out at last. 'But for now you can put on your jacket, button it up properly and take this F.I.R. book in to the A.D.I.G.'

His held-in ferocity seemed at last to have made an impact. Desai scrambled into his still damp jacket, did up all its buttons with fumbling fingers, took the F.I.R. book and tramped off.

Ghote watched him until he reached Tiger's door, gave it a knock that was more of a thump than a tap and plunged in – letting the memo attached to the wanted F.I.R. go leafing down on to the floor outside.

For a long moment Ghote stood looking at the sheet where it lay. Should he leave it there? Or wait till Desai emerged and tell him to pick it up and take it in, with all the chances of some disaster which that risked? Or should he retrieve the sheet himself and go into the office in Desai's wake?

Whatever he did was certain to bring a blast of rage from Tiger.

Best probably to do what was quickest.

He hurried along the passage, scooped up the sheet and entered the office with it.

Tiger was bent over papers he was examining and Desai was standing looking down at him with mouth-agape interest, the F.I.R. book still clutched in his heavy paw.

'Desai,' Ghote said, putting all the snap he could into his voice. 'Put down the F.I.R. Mr Kelkar wants and get out. At the double.'

'Oh.'

Desai emerged from his reverie, looking round as if he was unsure exactly where he was.

Then he realised.

'Oh. Oh, yes. F.I.R. book for A.D.I.G. Sahib. Take it in right away.'

He stood there.

'I told you to take it in,' Ghote said with forced patience, 'and then give it to the A.D.I.G.'

'Yes, Inspector. Give it. Right away, Inspector.'

Desai reached forward and attempted to place the book in front of Tiger, slap on top of what he was reading.

And, as he did so, the sleeve of his jacket just caught in the jutting hinge of the brass inkpot.

'Watch out, you –'

But Ghote's shout served only to precipitate the accident it was intended to avert. Desai jerked back his arm. The inkpot rose up with it, tilted over and sent a stream of new, beautifully black ink shooting aross the desk top and down on to Tiger Kelkar's immaculately pressed trousers.

At least the idiot realised what he had done. He emitted a sound something like the swirl of fast-gathering rainwater guggling down a crack in the earth and leapt backwards towards the door, his moony face plastered with fright.

And Tiger Kelkar, dark with fury, snatched up the inkpot and hurled it at him.

It hit him, too.

It just caught the side of his head and he went down as if he had been struck by a thunderbolt.

Ghote stood staring, first at Desai, lying like a great heap of mud on the floor, then at Tiger sitting at his desk, his expression switched in a moment from wild rage to blank incomprehension.

As well it might be, Ghote confusedly thought. What had happened was extraordinary. Extraordinary that the inkpot, seized in an instant and as quickly hurled, should have hit Desai at all. Extraordinary that having hit him the merest of glancing blows, so it seemed, it should have pole-axed the fellow like that.

Was he shamming? Was he putting on an act? It would be quite of a piece with his general idiocy of behaviour for him to exaggerate the effect of a touch of a blow like that. Except that he could never, dim-witted fool that he was, have reacted even half as quickly.

No, that hastily flung missile had actually knocked the chap out. No doubt about it.

Ghote stood while time seemed suspended staring at the inert mass of the man on the floor, too amazed at what had happened even to move.

It was Tiger who was the first to recover from the shock.

'Good God,' he said, shooting up from the desk and sending chair Number L1 toppling over backwards. 'I've laid the fool out.'

'Yes, sir,' Ghote managed to say.

He went over to where Desai lay, the empty inkpot neatly resting on the floor beside him. Kneeling, he turned the fellow's head to see exactly what damage had been done.

There did not seem to be much. The temple was marked

by a small gash. But the wound did not look particularly deep. Blood had gushed from it, jetting out on to the collar of the fellow's jacket, but now there was only a very little seeping slowly down his cheek.

But it was somehow seeping much more slowly than might be expected, too slowly, and a terrible thought flashed into Ghote's mind. Surely . . .

He grabbed Desai's wrist.

What he found there, or did not find, caused the flicker of thought he had had to grow and swell in his head like a cluster of buzzing blowflies in the first flush of a monsoon.

'Sir,' he said, steadily as his voice would allow. 'Sir, I am not altogether liking . . . Please, A.D.I.G. Sahib, come and examine this man.'

Tiger Kelkar crossed the room in two or three sharp strides and knelt beside the dumped, recumbent form. He lowered his head and placed an ear against the unmoving chest.

For several seconds he remained fixed where he was. Then he slowly straightened up and faced Ghote.

'You're right, Inspector,' he said. 'You're right.'

Ghote saw that his face had gone grey as the greyest hairs of the moustache above his iron-straight mouth.

'He has expired, sir, isn't it?' he said.

But he knew that was a question that did not need an answer.

3

For what seemed to Ghote a period of many, many minutes the two of them knelt there on either side of the dead man, looking at each other and stunned into speechlessness.

At first, coherent thoughts could hardly enter Ghote's mind. It was filled swampingly with the feeling that everything had in an instant been turned upside down. That nothing was as, moments before, it had been.

But then one notion made itself clear. And when, a little later, he became capable of examining the thought he could only wonder at what this catastrophic reversal had brought to the fore. It was, simply, that Tiger Kelkar was, of all the officers he had ever served under, the one he most admired.

He had never been wholly conscious of this before. He had hoped that he could contrive to act with something like the dedication and efficiency Tiger had shown, both back in the past in Bombay and now in the whirlwind days of his Inspection. He had wanted to be able to command in Tiger's way. But he felt now that he desired more to possess and use an anger that would make everything in his own work and, as well, the work of men under him sharply better.

Yes, he admired Tiger. Almost he seemed to worship him. Tiger was what he ought to become, however far off the goal.

Then another thought had come. Tiger, his worshipped Tiger, in one moment of rage, of the same anger that drove him and drove those to whom he gave orders to clean and castigate the evils of the world, Tiger had brought his whole career tumbling in ruins around him. Like a tall tower struck by a jaggedly thick blue-white spear of lightning he was suddenly a useless thing.

It was wrong. It should not be. It should not have been. But it was so, and nothing could change it.

Opposite him across Sergeant Desai's body, Tiger slowly got to his feet.

He stood looking down at the dead bulk on the floor, and Ghote, squatting back on his heels, looked up at the man he wished himself one day to be.

To have been – Ghote's thoughts raced – because now that man, that hero, was nothing other than the wreck of himself. It could not be otherwise. Whatever Tiger's intention had been, he had in rage seized a heavy object, thrown it at a subordinate and killed him. There could be nothing more for him in the police service, of which he had been until only a few instants ago an ornament and an inspiration.

Now, in all probability, what awaited him was a term in prison. Indian Police Code, Section 299, culpable homicide.

Evidently a similar train of thought must have been passing through Tiger's own mind. Suddenly now he barked out an order, his voice still sharp and unfaltering.

Old habits do not die straight away.

'Inspector, effect an arrest under Section 299.'

Ghote pushed himself to his feet, a darting ache shooting up the backs of his thighs.

He had no thought other than to obey Tiger's order. As he had always obeyed.

But the words he uttered, when they came, surprised even himself.

'No, sir. No, I will not do that.'

But he knew as soon as those words had passed his lips

27

that he meant them. He realised their implication, that he was going to abet Tiger in defying the law, and he knew still that he meant the words as deeply as any he had ever uttered.

He was not going to arrest Tiger as, a duty-bound police officer, he should. He was going somehow to get him out of the appalling situation he had fallen into. He was, he realised, more committed to Tiger, to anger-fuelled Tiger, than he was to the code of police conduct which he thought had entered into his very bones.

Yes, Tiger and his searching, saving anger had to be preserved, cost what it might.

But fury had flashed into Tiger's eyes, the same anger that would have sparked out before had any officer under him hesitated to obey an order. Then at once he knew he had lost his right to anger.

'Ghote,' he said, his voice now lacking all the bite it had had, his broad shoulders slumped. 'Ghote, man, you've got to do it. It – It's your duty. You're here. You saw what happened. Do it. Your duty.'

'No, Kelkar Sahib,' Ghote answered, the words now coming pouring out, as if in the traffic-blocked rush-hour streets of Bombay by some miracle a giant unseen hand had lifted out a clear path in front of him. 'No, Kelkar Sahib. There is something you are not knowing. You see, all during this evening I have one by one been sending off duty all personnels. They needed to get sleep, you see. Sir, there is no one here now but you and me, except for one sentry fellow outside.'

'What are you saying?'

Tiger looked to Ghote suddenly like some wild dacoit in the hills who, believing himself surrounded, had at the last moment seen a way out of the trap. He looked – somehow his very hair had become lank and dishevelled – as if he only half believed what he was seeing and yet could not distrust his eyes.

'Sir, I am saying that there has been no witness to the

event, except only myself. There is no one in the station to have heard anything even.'

Abruptly the thought of Shinde came into Ghote's head. How far would the fellow have had to walk at this time of night before finding somewhere to buy that fool Desai his single cigarette? Would he come back into the station at any moment?

But even if he did, almost certainly it would not matter. Shinde, for whatever reason, had his eyes-melting devotion. He would, if it was asked of him, see nothing, hear nothing, know nothing. No matter how the deception outraged his better feelings, he would not lift up a sword.

He gulped twice and continued.

'Sir, if we are only somewhat lucky we can make this all look as if it was something altogether different.'

'Different?'

Tiger Kelkar was still the bewildered brigand.

'Yes, sir, different. Sir, there is no reason why this man should have been killed here. He should not have been within the station at all, sir. Many hours past I was sending him to his quarter.'

Now, slowly the light of understanding was creeping into Tiger's wild eyes.

'What exactly are you telling me, Ghote?'

'Sir, this death, we both know, was the most unfortunate of accidents only. Well, sir, why should it not have occurred as the result of an accident that was happening elsewhere?'

'But where, man? And why?'

'Sir, that has already come to me. The fellow was for ever boasting, sir, that he was a Number One fine swimmer. Sir, there is Lake Helena. Its shore is not far from here.'

'Lake Helena? You're suggesting that somehow we should contrive to make it look as if . . . as if the fellow got himself into the lake and – what? – drowned himself there? Hit his head?'

'Yes, sir. It could be done. If we are acting quickly, A.D.I.G. Sahib.'

Ghote cursed himself then for having let Tiger's rank slip out. Would it remind him who he was? What his duty was, or what until only minutes before it had been?

It seemed to. For a moment Tiger drew himself up, straight-backed as ever, and a hint of his old fiery anger blazed up.

But it was replaced almost at once. By a look of pure longing.

And that won. Tiger Kelkar stooped, picked up the brass inkpot and put it back exactly where it had been on his desk.

The prospect, however chancy, however slim, of being once more all that he was meant to be was too much for him.

'But, Ghote, why on earth should this fellow, why should anybody, get themselves into the lake on a night like this?'

And, as if to reinforce his point, at that moment the steady rain beating down on the solid tiled roof above them broke into a tattoo of frenzied fist-blows.

But the answer to Tiger's question had already come to Ghote in that single moment when the whole idea, the traffic jam of other thoughts ahead mysteriously cleared, had appeared in his head.

'Sir,' he replied, 'Desai was a damn fool only.'

'Well?'

'Sir, he was notorious. He was boasting always of his swimming powers, taking up bets each and every day. Sir, it is not at all unlikely that he would have got someone to put him up with a bet to swim across Lake Helena in the uttermost middle of the first monsoon downpour.'

'But – But – Let me think. The bet, Ghote, the bet. No one can come forward to say he made it. They do not exist.'

Ghote felt the ideas springing up in his mind, uncurling one after another like new growth in this lush monsoon time.

'Sir, no one would come forward.'

'Exactly, man. There is no one.'

'No, sir, no. Kindly listen. If you had taken up such a bet with a fellow like Desai and he had gone and done that thing, attempted to swim across Lake Helena in such a storm as this and had then deceased, would you afterwards admit?'

Tiger thought for just a moment.

'No, by God,' he said, 'I'd keep my damn mouth shut for ever.'

He gave Ghote a look. His eyes were shining with something like their old vigour. There might have been a party of gold smugglers coming to a rendezvous somewhere round Bombay and he waiting in command of half a dozen armed police to seize them.

'Right,' he snapped. 'Which way do we go with him?'

'By the back entrance,' Ghote said. 'It looks on to the police lines of course, but after such a beehive activity as you have been making today, sir, no one would be in any way awake.'

Tiger smiled then. A short grim smile, but a smile.

'Right. Make sure the coast outside here's clear and we'll have a bloody good try.'

Ghote walked round the lifeless thing between himself and the door and stepped out. The peon's bench immediately opposite was still unoccupied. Plainly poor Shinde had had to go far in the sheeting rain to find that cigarette Desai had so high-handedly sent him to buy. Or perhaps like a sensible fellow he had taken shelter.

He went quietly along to the entrance hall. There was not a sound nor a sign of anyone having unexpectedly come in.

So all seemed to be well.

He turned back to tell Tiger.

And as he reached the office door the full enormity of what he was doing came upon him. Desai was dead. He who had been living, a living, breathing fool, was now no more. Lifeless flesh. But that flesh had been a man, a man born of woman. With a wife. But, no. No, he remembered, Desai mercifully had managed to remain unmarried. But he might well have a mother still alive. A mother deprived in one instant of her son, and perhaps a father now with no one to perform his funeral rites. And that son, that man, had been unlawfully killed. And he, an officer of police, was busy condoning the killing.

Caught up as he had been in the sudden opening out of his plan, he had let it run on and on. Seeing suddenly a way he could render his admired superior the greatest possible assistance in his hour of greatest need, he had without thought put forward addition after addition to his first idea. And now there seemed to be no going back. Tiger had seized on the plan the way a hungry dog might snatch a haunch of juicy meat and run off, and there was no stopping him any more.

He felt sick.

For a moment he held on to the post of the door. A thick and greasy sweat broke out down his spine and over his shoulders and neck.

But there could indeed be no going back. He had put his plan to Tiger and he was being carried along now like a floating piece of stick in a rain-filled nullah, swirled and jerked and tossed onwards and onwards.

And one half of him did not want to go back. His plan might yet save Tiger, and Tiger was worth saving. He was worth saving if anyone in the whole police service was worth saving. He had years in front of him yet, years in which, with his vigour and his scorching anger, he would drive the service into ever better achievements. Tiger was a good man. An example. And it had been given to himself to erase the one terrible moment of fury and its single unforeseeable consequence that otherwise would end Tiger's career for ever.

He drew in a breath, harsh and sucking, opened the door and slipped back in.

'All clear, sir,' he said.

In the time he had been out of the room, hardly more than

two minutes, it was plain that Tiger had regained much of his old spirit. His shoulders were straight again, the look of unflagging determination was back on his blade-sharp face. He had even thought to pass a hand over his hair.

'Right,' he said, 'I've mopped up those spots of blood and ink on the floor, so we can go right away. You take the shoulders. I'll take the legs. Jump to it, man.'

Ghote had hesitated, a wave of his appalled feelings briefly returning at Tiger's unsparing references to the body on the floor. But the very decisiveness of the last words banished all doubts.

He stooped, slipped his hands under Desai's inert back and up through the armpits. Tiger at the same time grasped the legs beneath the knees.

'Right. Up.'

Ghote heaved. The weight of the body was somehow much more than he had expected. He blew out a snort of air from puffed cheeks. His whole chest strained and expanded. There came a tiny ripping sound and he knew that one of the buttons on his over-tight best uniform had popped.

He heard it tinkle and roll as it struck the floor.

'Right,' Tiger barked.

Moving awkwardly backwards, Ghote steered their heavy burden through the door and began staggering along the passage outside, dank and echoing in the silence of the deserted building.

They arrived at the rear door and Ghote, managing to keep the body off the floor with one arm and his hip, got it open and peered out into the darkness.

There was nothing there but the unending sploshing of the rain and, accompanying it, the incessant tweet-tweet-tweet of cicadas everywhere, like so many ever-ringing tiny telephones.

'Nobody to be seen, sir,' he grunted, turning his head back towards Tiger.

They lurched out into the warm downpour. The ground

was already puddled and slidy. Ghote had taken only some six or seven steps when his right foot slipped under him and the heavy body, already streaming with rainwater, almost escaped his grasp. He came to a halt.

'Get on, man, get on,' Tiger snapped.

Grimly, sweating at every pore, Ghote resumed his backwards march. The rain beat down on his head and soon there was not a dry inch of clothing on him.

He found himself, as step by step he went along, recalling bitterly the start of the monsoon in his childhood days when the coming of the rain had seemed sudden sheer bliss. Then they had all rushed out into it, rejoicing in the coolness sluicing down on them and in the fragrant odours rising up almost at once from the parched earth. The smallest children, often entirely naked, would fling themselves flat in the rapidly forming puddles and kick up their little legs in delight, and even the staidest of the elders would run out, lift arms high to the streaming water and shout with the best 'Ho, ho, ho, ho.' In those days, too, he had even believed the unending telephone-shrill noise of the cicadas was the sound coming from the high-above diamond-twinkling stars.

How different it all was now.

They staggered on. Desai's body seemed to get heavier with every awkward back-pacing step.

How far was it to the lake? In that first dazzling moment of hope he had told Tiger it was not all that distant. He had felt then it was not. But it was. It must be at least half a mile.

'Sir,' he forced out, between gasps for breath, 'I do not think we can do this. It is still a long, long way.'

'Nonsense, man,' Tiger responded at once. 'The job's got to be done, and we're the only ones to do it.'

There was anger fizzing in every syllable.

'Yes, sir,' Ghote said.

For a little he contrived to move onwards, even going at a slightly better pace. But the weight of the body tugging at his hands and the ever-increasing wetness of Desai's cotton uniform was making the burden slip nearer and nearer the slimy, puddle-pocked ground.

At last Tiger must have seen what was happening.

'Stop, man, and put him down,' he snapped. 'Take a better grip. Put some guts into it.'

Ghote let Desai's bulk slide the last few inches to the ground and straightened his already aching back.

But Tiger's taunt had not discouraged him. Instead it had made him think. Hard.

'Sir,' he said, 'I believe we must take some transportation.'

'Trans –'

Crackling fury was in the half-uttered word.

But, before Tiger could let forth the yet more ferocious firing that was plainly on the way, Ghote's whirring brain produced a concrete suggestion.

'Sir, we have just only passed the bicycle stable. Sir, we could take a bicycle and use that.'

A tiny pause in the rain-splattering darkness.

'Good man. Good. Is the place locked?'

'Yes, sir. Regulations, A.D.I.G. Sahib. But I can be getting the key in one jiffy.'

'Then what are you waiting for? At the double, man. At the double.'

Ghote pelted off, slithering and sliding, back to the station, went in and ran along to the key-board, seized the bicycle stable key from its labelled hook – he had seen to it in his first week that all the labels were renewed and each key put in its proper place – and hurried back.

Ahead on the stone floor of the passage he saw the wet marks his feet had made coming in. For a moment a fear entered his mind that somehow they would betray what was happening. But he dismissed the thought at once. Long before anyone, except perhaps the faithful Shinde, came this way any marks would have dried into nothingness.

He ran out into the rain again, made his way to the stable,

heaved a heavy regulation bicycle from its stand and pushed it hurriedly along to where Tiger was waiting.

'Good man.'

Together they hoisted Desai's awkward bulk up on to the machine and got it more or less into place, the stomach drooping down on either side of the saddle, the top of the chest across the handlebars, one arm dangling at each side.

It was not an easy matter to get moving. But after a trial or two they managed to hit on a system that enabled them to make reasonable progress. Ghote went first, one hand behind him grasping the bicycle's handlebar at its centre underneath Desai's throat. Spreading his fingers as wide as he could, he was able, just, to keep the front wheel of the machine straight. Tiger at the rear provided the motive power.

But it was still a long way to the lake, and part of the journey of necessity would take them through the outskirts of the town.

4

At least after they had struggled along on their miserable, muscle-straining journey for some ten minutes more the rain began to slacken. Aware that he was now able to see further ahead, Ghote looked upwards and found that the unbroken cloud had thinned and a full moon, orangey and dim, was just visible.

But they had reached the part of the town which they could not avoid going through, a scatter of large houses with views over the lake a quarter of a mile or so away.

And almost at once there came from in front of one of the first of the houses a shrill whistle-blast from the chowkidar on guard there. The long, plaintive note was answered by another from the next watchman where the houseowner had invested in such a precaution. And then, one by one, half a dozen others took up the signal, more and more faintly each time, and back in answer eventually came the rattle of bamboo lathis on the ironwork of gates.

Ghote shivered with dismay. He had thought that on such a night the chowkidars would be huddled away out of the wet, out of sight and in all probability safely dozing. But evidently the slackening-off in the rain had roused the first of them and now he had woken all the others along the road ahead.

Tiger, at the first sound, had ceased to push their cumbersome burden. Ghote stood now looking almost desperately from side to side.

And at last he saw what he hoped he might find.

'Sir,' he whispered, 'there is a back-lane just there. I think we must be taking it. It would be longer but safer also.'

'Lead on, Inspector. This is your territory.'

Ghote felt then a glimmer of pride. Yes, this was his territory, short though the time had been since he had acquired it. But at least he knew enough about it to be able to help Tiger, his hero.

'Push, please,' he whispered.

Moving yet more awkwardly they succeeded in turning the heavy bicycle and its yet heavier burden and making their way into the entrance to the lane. The ground under their feet now was even more slippery than it had been when they were on the road, and their progress, squelching and sliding, became yet slower, especially as the high walls of the compounds on either side made it almost impossible to see where they were going.

Head down, grunting with effort, Ghote plunged on.

Then at last he was able to make out, scarcely lighter than the walls to either side, the sky ahead where the lane came to an end and, a couple of hundred yards further on, lay the lake.

He plunged his head down once more and forced his legs to stride out.

The droning buzz of some heavy flying insect, brought into activity by the wetness, sounded out in the still air.

And, a couple of minutes later, the faintly glimmering black water of the lake was in front of them, its surface now hardly disturbed by the rain which had become little more than a drizzle.

'Good man,' said Tiger Kelkar once more.

And once more Ghote felt a warm surge of pride. Yes, he was helping Tiger. He had already helped him more than a little. And if what it was that he had to do in order to save him entirely was a desecration which he would never have believed himself capable of, well, the cause was as good as it could be. Should they manage to complete this business as well as they had begun it, Tiger tomorrow and for the rest of his career would be the dynamic, fierily fuelled police officer that the force needed, that the whole of society needed.

'Right,' came Tiger's voice in the dark, sharper now that they were clear of the houses, 'we'll have to get it out into decently deep water.'

For a moment then Ghote's revulsion came flooding back. It. It. That was what had become of Desai, boasting idiot though he had been. It. That son of a mother. That man.

'Wake yourself up,' Tiger snapped. 'Is there anywhere nearby where the water is deep at the lake's edge?'

With a jerk Ghote brought himself back to the present.

'No, sir, no,' he answered. 'I am not thinking there is. Naturally I have not had time in my stay here for many saunterings by the side of these waters, but from what I have seen all the banks slope as gently as here.'

He looked down at his feet. It was possible, just, to make out in the diffused moonlight that this was a spot which people visited in some numbers, either to bathe or to wash clothes. The hollows their feet had made long before in the mud had not been entirely obliterated by the beating rain of one night.

'Well, man, are there no boats? Look alive. Scout along the shore and see what you can find.'

Impelled by the force behind the order, Ghote set off, slipping and sliding in the dark.

Oh God, he thought, what if I should tread on a snake? They always come out when the monsoon starts. If I get bitten, that will put an end to the whole thing. And it will look worse if they see Tiger was trying to cover up what he had done.

But almost at once he glimpsed, looming out of the moon-diffused darkness, the shape of a fisherman's boat.

He hurried forward. The craft had been pulled up on to the bank and secured by a rope tied to a tree root. There were, of course, no oars. But he thought that between them they ought to be able to propel the vessel far enough out for Tiger's purposes.

With chilled, almost useless fingers he tackled the knot in the sodden rope.

When he got back to where he had left Tiger, dragging the boat after him through the water without actually having to walk in it himself, he came to an appalled halt. Tiger was kneeling beside the recumbent mass of Desai's body and with something heavy in his right hand was delivering blow after blow to the head.

For a moment Ghote thought that, under the strain of events, Tiger had actually gone mad, that the anger which had always fuelled him had burst uncontrollably out. But almost at once he realised what it was that he was doing, and Tiger's words as soon as he stepped forward confirmed his guess.

'Right, I've just pretty well disguised the wound by giving it a few good biffs. But we've got to do a bit more than that.'

'Sir?'

'If we're going to make it look at all as if the chap drowned, we're going to have to get some water into him somehow. You remember the Police Manual. First thing to check in a case of suspected drowning, water in the lungs and internal cavities.'

'Yes, sir, I am well remembering.'

'Good. Well, what we'll have to use, I think, is the pump from the bicycle. It's by no means ideal. But if we can provide some sort of evidence it will have to do. With any luck the body will be pretty well decomposed before it's discovered.'

Ghote swallowed. And it was thanks to him, he thought, that the bicycle he had taken had got a pump on it. When he had inspected the bicycle stable during his first days at the station he had seen that hardly any of the machines were properly equipped and he had issued an order that all deficiencies were to be made good.

He took the pump from its clips, went down to the water's edge and filled it.

'Good,' said Tiger. 'Now I'll work the arms to expand the lungs and you can squirt in. At least that'll get some water in somewhere.'

The business – Ghote had to refill the pump five or six times – took a full quarter of an hour and was appallingly miserable to carry out. Flies by the hundred had scented out the dead flesh, or perhaps just the living sweat, and they buzzed and whined round, settling time and again on per-spiration-soaked forehead and neck, on face and lips. Even when Tiger was at last satisfied that the maximum effect had been achieved he still found more to do.

'Got to get the fellow stripped. He wouldn't go swimming, even in this weather, in uniform.'

So, heaving and tugging, they pulled the clothes off the big body until they were down to the undershorts. Then they lifted it up once more, yet harder to handle now that it was naked and slippery, and carried it down to the fisherman's boat. At last they were able to push the frail craft out and scramble in, one at each end. Their combined weight brought the lake water to within two or three inches of the sides. But Tiger was undismayed.

'Right,' he said. 'Paddle.'

With no more motive power than their cupped hands they set off. It was very still. The rain had now ceased altogether, although thin cloud covered the sky. Slowly the shoreline disappeared, and it became impossible to tell how fast or how slowly they were progressing.

Somewhere in the distance a jackal barked, harshly, once.

Ghote, momentarily mistaking the sound for an angry exclamation from Tiger behind him, redoubled his rate of paddling.

'Steady, you fool,' Tiger snapped.

On they went, faint ripples spreading out to either side of the boat's prow.

Then at last Tiger called a halt.

'All right, we'll risk it here. Now, be careful how you tip him out or you'll have us both swimming for it.'

'Yes, sir.'

With much painful rocking of the little boat and with water more than once slopping in, they manoeuvred the inert mass between them until at last they had it balanced on the craft's side while they each leant precariously in the other direction. Then, inch by inch, they toppled it into the water.

The great rubbery body did not, as Ghote had for some reason expected, sink at once out of sight. Instead it floated face down beside them.

'Sir,' he said, panic-touched for an instant, 'it is not sinking. It will not sink.'

'Of course it won't, you fool. Not for five days or more. Don't you remember what you learnt at police college? But unless we're very unlucky it should be decently decomposed before it's found.'

'Yes, sir.'

Then once more they set off paddling. But now, with the boat riding higher in the water, it did not take anything like as long before they felt the prow nudge its way into the mud of the bank.

Ghote, sploshing ashore, let the thought of oblivion-bringing sleep invade his mind. But Tiger's voice ripped into the night air again.

'Get this boat back where it belongs, man, and then you'd

better return the bicycle. I'm going to make my way to the Inspection Bungalow and see if I can get in without drawing attention. I advise you to do the same wherever your quarter is. But if you do disturb anyone tell them, in a way they won't dare contradict, that it's not midnight yet.'

Ghote's spirits sank. So much still between him and the blotting-out of sleep. But, impelled once more by Tiger's vigour, he set out dragging the boat by its rope towards the place where he had found it.

Behind him he heard Tiger briskly squelching his way up the muddy bank.

He found the tree root to which the boat had been tied in the dark by tripping full-length over it. But even lying flat on his face with the rotting smell of mud sharp in his nostrils, he felt nothing but relief that at least the first of the remaining complications had been dealt with. If only the others went with no more trouble, his gift to Tiger would be complete.

The gift of liberty to go on acting with as much vigour as he had just been showing, with as much effective anger, to the benefit of all.

It would have been worth it then.

He rose to his feet, got the boat tied up and hurried back to where they had left the bicycle.

There he came upon Desai's clothes, strewn where they had let them drop as one by one they had peeled them from the slobbery body.

What should he do with them? Even someone as idiotic as Desai would not have left them here while he swum the lake for his bet in the middle of such a downpour as there had been earlier on. Best to take them with him and perhaps tomorrow spot out a likely place where Desai might have put them in the dry. Or perhaps it would be best just to destroy them, with that tell-tale dark splodge of blood on the jacket.

He bundled them together and went to heave up the bicycle.

Then he remembered the pump.

He found it after a few minutes' frantic search among the foot-pocks in the mud and clipped it back in its proper place, allowing a small warm feeling to lodge in his head that things might at last be going to go wholly right.

And it seemed as if this optimism was justified. It took him only minutes to speed back on the bicycle down the lane that had taken them so long to tramp along wheeling the body. At the bicycle stable he was able to put the machine back into its rack with little sign that it had ever been away. Then he hurried in at the station's rear entrance hugging the bundle of Desai's clothes to his chest.

How long had it been since he and Tiger had staggered out this way with the lolling body between them? He looked at his watch. Past 2.30. No wonder he felt bone-weary.

Cautiously he made his way along the passage. The warm night air, now that the rain had ceased, had dried his dripping uniform and even his shoes as he had swept along on the bicycle enough for him not to be making too many give-away marks on the floor. And, thank goodness, he had even managed to scrape off a lot of the mud. He turned the corner.

And there, patiently dozing on his bench, was the faithful Shinde.

He had forgotten entirely that the fellow would have returned. And, yes, carefully placed on the bench beside him was the single cigarette Desai had sent him out to buy.

He sidled back round the corner. Had he woken Shinde? Would the fellow come looking for him?

Too anxious to be angry with himself, he stood, clutching the bundle of blood-marked clothes, and waited for the sound of footsteps.

Nothing happened.

He let out a great sigh of held breath.

But the clothes. He would have to go past Shinde's bench to put the bicycle stable key back – Why, oh why, had he been so insistent that every key should be returned immediately after use? – and he could not do that clutching this bundle.

What to do? What to do?

And the answer came.

The Muddamal Room. Its door was just behind him, and in it there were stacks and piles of lost and detained property. There would be dozens of articles of clothing among them. Had it not been Desai himself who earlier in this long, long night had said there were plenty of hangers in the place? Where better to hide clothes than among other clothes? And then he could rescue them at some convenient time in the next day or two and finally get rid of them.

He opened the door, slipped in, stuffed the bundle at the back of one of the slatted wooden shelves behind the boxy shape of a public-address loudspeaker, doubtless confiscated, and quickly left.

He paused for a moment outside deciding how he should act.

Then, banging his shoes down noisily as he could, he went back down the passage and round the corner.

'Shinde,' he exclaimed. 'You are here still?'

The peon jumped to his feet.

'Sahib, so sorry, sahib,' he stammered. 'I am getting for Sergeant Desai one cigarette. But something you are wanting?'

'No, there is nothing. Sergeant Desai went long ago. Here, I'll pay for the cigarette. You smoke it.'

Shinde's eyes glowed with absurd gratitude.

Now is the time, Ghote thought. If I am to gain his collaboration, as I must, then this is the moment to do it.

'Shinde,' he said, 'you have not seen me just now. Understand? If anyone is asking, at any time, say I left with the A.D.I.G. Sahib before midnight. Before midnight, understand?'

'Oh yes, Inspector Sahib,' Shinde said, straightening himself up and giving his best splay-fingered salute.

Quite plainly he was not going to question whatever it was this cigarette-donating god chose to tell him.

'So go home now,' Ghote said. 'And I left before midnight, remember.'

He got a second terrific, fingers-wide salute, and then the peon scuttled happily away, carefully stowing Desai's cigarette into his shirt pocket.

Ghote stood for a moment in thought. Had he done everything necessary now?

No. No, there was one tiny thing that had to be looked to yet.

He turned, opened Inspector Khan's door and from the floor picked up the button from his own uniform which had burst off at the moment he had first strained to lift the dead weight of Desai.

It could hardly have been a possible clue to what had happened. But with it safely in his pocket he felt he could finally relax.

5

It was not long before Ghote was able to flop down on to his straw mattress, prickly as ever, in Shivram Patel's house. He had made his way there wearily tramping, crossing the big neglected compound suddenly prey to fears that it must, muddy and soaked now like the lake shore, be a playground for snakes, but coming at last to the tall old door of the house. There he had tapped and tapped again with the padlock chain till the solitary old servant had heard and come and lifted the door-bar.

He had not forgotten then Tiger's instructions, and had at once complained of being kept waiting 'at almost midnight'. The bleary-eyed old servant had made no objection to the claim, and Ghote had gone up to his isolated room, pleased in so far as he was capable of feeling anything at all that this one last piece had been put into place in Tiger's alibi.

As at last he had sunk into sleep a curious thought, or even vision, had hovered for a moment in his mind. He had seen himself as God Krishna, no less, blue-bodied and beautiful of limb as in the calendar pictures, holding aloft, umbrella-like, steep Mount Godharvan so as to protect from the fury of the terrible storm above, not all the people of the village of Braj, but simply Tiger, a harassed and momentarily anger-deprived Tiger.

Next morning he managed to get up and get himself down to the station well on time. Much as he had expected, however, Tiger was there before him, spruce and vigorous as always in a uniform that showed no sign of any black ink-stain.

But, something he had not at all expected, he found, when on his way to the office he made his customary first-thing check of the Daily Disposition Chart, that Sergeant Desai's name figured in the list of those due for their weekly 'off'.

So, he reflected, in all probability he himself, and Tiger, would have a 24-hour respite before questions began to be asked and Desai's disappearance would come to light, with all the consequences that would follow.

He was not sorry. After the nightmare events he had endured he hardly felt capable of another bout of lying and evasion, frequently though he told himself that the first one had had to be gone through. Those lies and deceitful action, however horrible, had all been worthwhile for Tiger's sake. But a respite was more than welcome. The umbrella of Mount Godharvan was in danger of tilting in Krishna's hands.

Tiger he had found not only spruce but already hard at work at Inspector Khan's desk, the brass inkpot in its place in front of him as if it had never left it.

'Ah, Inspector, good morning. I've finished with this F.I.R. book now. Tell your peon he can come in and collect it.'

'Yes, sir,' Ghote said.

So this was how it was to be. As if what had happened had not happened. Surely no one but Tiger would dare to impose his will on events quite so fiercely. What a man. Yes, it really had been worth it all to keep him at work. And he, too, would play out the rest of his part. However many doubts came upon him, he would fight them off. Turn time back. Make what had happened in this very room not eight hours before cease to have been. Yes. He would do it. For Tiger.

'You'll see some ink got split on the book, but the F.I.R. itself escaped.'

'Yes, sir.'

'Oh, and Ghote.'

'Sir?'

'I shall finish Inspection by 1800 hours and be leaving for Pune straight away.'

'Yes, sir. Very good, sir.'

'And, Ghote, I see no reason why I should not tell you. I shall be giving you a reasonably good chit. The station is in good order, on the whole. Some deficiencies. But I understand most of them are Inspector Khan's responsibility, not yours.'

'Yes, sir. Thank you, sir.'

And, beyond being present, stiffly at attention and saluting, when the A.D.I.G. took his departure – on the stroke of 1800 hours – Ghote hardly saw Tiger Kelkar again.

Almost as soon as the jeep with Tiger's erect figure in the back had disappeared into the evening's wind-swirled rain he put himself off duty, consumed a hasty meal of soggy parathas at a tumbledown eating-stall called the Elite Hotel and headed back to Shivram Patel's prickly mattress. He was weary in every limb, incapable of any thought. He had a lot of sleep to catch up on.

By the following day, however, he felt completely recovered. The aches in the muscles of his back and arms, jabbing reminders during the last hours of Tiger's Inspection of what had happened the night before, had eased away. He found himself even looking forward to the weeks ahead. Tiger had decreed that the ordeal they had shared should be blotted out of existence. So be it. There was work to be done and he would need his best energies. Better to tackle it unencumbered.

First of all, of course, but perhaps not for an hour or so yet,

49

there would be the business of Desai's disappearance. But now, he felt, he could deal even with that. He would bark out orders in true Tiger style that the man had to be found. He would see that the investigation was pressed forward hard as it would go. The full-scale bandobust he would set in motion would be a model of sharp efficiency.

He entered the station, acknowledging smartly the sentry's salute, and made his way to his office. His office once again. He opened the door briskly, thinking only about which routine task he would get down to first.

And there at the desk was someone he had never seen before, in uniform with an inspector's three stars on the shoulder tabs of his shirt. He looked at the black plastic name-tag above the top pocket. *M. A. Khan.*

'Good God,' he said, 'it is Inspector Khan. I thought you were ill itself.'

'It must be Inspector Ghote. Heard it was you who had taken over. Was ill, of course. But fit as a fiddle again now. Fit as a fiddle.'

Ghote stood there in the doorway, blinking.

Had the fellow weeks ago got wind somehow that an Inspection was coming? And had he craftily contrived to get a certificate from the local Medical Officer that he was unfit for duty? It was possible, definitely possible. But this sudden return when the storm had blown over must mean, good heavens, that his own stay in the Town of Difficulties was at an end.

It was fine news. If hard to take in. No longer would he have to battle with the errors and omissions that still remained from Khan's earlier days. No longer would he have to suffer the misery of life in Shivram Patel's empty echoing house. And he had eaten the last greasy paratha from the Elite Hotel stall.

That other thing, too, what had happened two nights ago, the burden of that and its consequences had, surely, been lifted altogether now from his shoulders.

He had in one instant been relieved of all the charade of finding Desai missing and setting up an Inquiry. Desai, that poor idiotic fool whose dignity in death he had sacrificed for the continuing existence as a senior police officer of Tiger Kelkar was now a problem for Inspector Khan, with his by no means formidable powers.

And that, after all, was probably a very good thing. An extra piece of luck. For himself. For Tiger.

'Well,' he said, slowly coming to, 'I will be off back to Bombay then.'

'Yes,' Inspector Khan answered cheerfully. 'Yes, goodbye then, Inspector. And thanks, man, for holding the fort.'Bye.'

So, before noon that day Ghote was on a train taking him back to his old life, his proper life.

Now once more he would be doing the work for which he felt he was especially fitted. Now he would not be battling with the petty daily tasks of a backwood police station. Instead he would be tackling real crime. There would be put in front of him – often in all too great abundance – the results of wrongdoing. A murdered body sometimes, sometimes a person of influence robbed of jewels or money, perhaps a case under Indian Penal Code Section 232, counterfeiting. Any sort of serious wrongdoing. And then, by God, he would find the criminals, and he would get up cases against them that no clever defence counsel, no do-gooder from the People's Union for Civil Liberties, could find one hole in.

At home, too, his life would settle down on its proper track. He would return after a busy day and Protima would be there with food for him, not the greasy parathas and poor tea of the Elite Hotel but the food he liked, cooked the way he liked it, cooked as only Protima, his loved, elegant and – yes, all right – sometimes spikily determined wife, could prepare and cook it.

There would be Ved, too, to watch over and guide as a father should, and, with bated breath, to let find his own way a little in the dangerous world. A boy learning and grasping the facts of things, the facts sometimes prickly and producing their pinpoints of blood, sometimes seemingly stiff and unbending, but, once mastered, able to be turned to good account. Ved, his son, his heir. Perhaps one day like himself to become a police officer. Even to become a better police officer than he himself was. The boy was clever enough, and he had enough energy. Perhaps if he could instill in him bit by bit that ferocity that Tiger possessed, that long-lasting cleansing anger, his son might at the last become the Commissioner of Bombay Police. His son.

The train clattered onwards.

Vigatpore and everything that had happened there began to seem only a sort of dream. The whole time of his stay was something he could forget about. He would forget about it.

And so he did. Within days of coming back to Bombay the place seemed to recede into a far distance. His stay there became on a par with the period he had spent at police college when he had first joined the service, a block of time out of his life, not altogether pleasant and entirely different from anything that had gone before it or had come after it. It was a period he seldom thought about at all, and then only as if the things that had happened then had happened to somebody else.

Back at home now, he hardly mentioned Vigatpore. He had written regular letters to Protima, and there was nothing to add to them. Except of course what had taken place on the night of June 24, and he had no intention of even hinting at that. Nor was there anything at Headquarters to bring that night back to his mind. He found on his desk tag-ends of work from before he had been transferred. Soon other inquiries, too many of them, landed in front of him. They kept him busy from first thing in the morning till late at night.

And from Vigatpore he heard nothing.

Now and again the absence of any news crossed his mind as faintly worrying. He would have liked to have known, especially in the first week or two after his return, what had happened. But there was no particular reason why he should have been informed of Desai's disappearance. It had, to all intents and purposes, taken place after his term of duty there. And what, of course, he must never do was to ask any questions himself.

So gradually the whole business, terrible though it had been, faded from his mind.

6

Time passed. The monsoon, which lingered on that year with occasional storms even as late as October, catching out the umbrellaless crowds and sending them scurrying with folded newspapers over their heads, eventually ended. The pleasant months of winter came. And went. The broiling, humid days of summer arrived.

And then one sun-crackling day in April Ghote was summoned by the Assistant Commissioner, Crime Branch. He thought it was in order to be given some more than usually important assignment and went up to the A.C.P.'s office with no more than a prickle of anxiety.

There was a young woman sitting in one of the three chairs drawn up in a marshalled row in front of the A.C.P.'s desk. She was a person of about thirty, serious-looking, with large hornrim spectacles, wearing a rather modern sari in little squares of bright scarlet with alternate designs of a lotus and a swastik in each.

Ghote made some quick, instinctive assessments, a matter of second nature. Educated, yes. A graduate, in all probability. Gujarati, of course, from the way she wore that sari. And, unless she was a Muslim, a married woman, her forehead marked by a crimson tika.

He came to a halt at the side of the A.C.P.'s desk and clicked heels in salute.

'Ah, Ghote,' the A.C.P. said. 'I want you to meet Mrs Desai.'

'Yes, sir,' he answered, the common name of Desai meaning at that moment nothing in particular to him.

'Mrs Desai, Ghote, is the sister-in-law of one Sergeant Desai S.R., a former member of the Maharastra Police, who, I believe, served under you during your secondment to Vigatpore last year.'

Then, with an explosive impact like the splitting of a dam wall, all the events of that night of June 24 poured back into his mind. Now at last, he supposed, he was to learn just what had been the aftermath of the plot he and Tiger had put into action. Now he was to hear the full implications of that instant of decision back in Vigatpore when he had put himself on Tiger's side once and for all.

He barely managed to get out a hoarse 'Yes, sir.'

'Mrs Desai, Ghote, has certain anxieties concerning the death of her brother-in-law, and it occurred to me that since you were right here in the building and had been at Vigatpore also about the time poor Desai drowned, you might be able to set those anxieties at rest here and now. And no more said about them.'

The A.C.P. darted a look at Mrs Desai, Sergeant Desai's sister-in-law, his bhabhi, that to Ghote's eye spoke of an urgent desire to be rid of a nuisance.

And he had learnt something himself of which till now, of necessity, he had been ignorant. Desai had, after all, been believed to have drowned. Well and good. All that Tiger and he had been through on that fearful night seemed to have been worthwhile. Krishna's mountain umbrella still protected the ornament of the police service. And there was, after all, no one anywhere who could know what it was that the two of them had actually done that night.

He felt a surge of confidence.

'If I can help in any way, sir,' he said, 'though I left Vigatpore before this sad thing happened. I am learning of it only now.'

But the red-saried, horn-rimmed bhabhi had ignored all this. Her eyes behind her thick spectacles were fixed on the A.C.P. And they were flashing in anger.

'But that is the whole question,' she stormed. 'My husband has all along been altogether unable to believe that his brother drowned. From his earliest boyhood that man was a magnificent swimmer. He could not have drowned.'

'But, madam,' the A.C.P. answered, with a placating wave of his hand, 'as I understand it the – er – event took place when there was a first-class storm in progress, the first of the monsoon. Isn't that so, Ghote?'

'Well, yes, sir,' Ghote hastened to agree. 'If poor Desai did expire during the first storm of the monsoon, that was just only before my posting to Vigatpore ended. And most certainly that was a very, very wild night.'

Desai's bhabhi ignored him.

'No,' she said, 'there is scientific evidence also. I am graduate in biology, let me remind. I am fully capable of judging such things.'

Scientific evidence, Ghote thought with sudden dull dismay. Had Tiger then got it wrong? Was it not possible to get water into the lungs, however well they had succeeded in pumping it into the internal cavities?

'I have seen Government Medical Officer's report, remember,' the bhabhi went on, her gaze lifted to the A.C.P. like a horseman's steed scenting battle. 'No sign of blueness of nails due to asphyxia. Not one mention. And, let me tell you, death by drowning is death from asphyxia. That you were not knowing, were you?'

She gave the A.C.P. a look of rich triumph, and Ghote could not suppress a dart of admiration. Here was a woman, not all that old and, even if she was a graduate, certainly no more than just middle class, and yet she was standing up to as authoritative a figure as the Assistant Commissioner, Crime Branch, in his own office, at the heart of Bombay Police Headquarters. A girl full of guts.

How different from poor, foolish, moonily grinning Desai. No doubt the brother, her husband, must be a fellow in much the same mould, which was why it was she who had taken up the case.

And she had a right to. If, it seemed, Desai's death had not left a bereaved mother and a father with no one to break his skull on the funeral pyre, all the same it had left one brother without another. His own act of deceit, and Tiger's, had covered up the truth of that loss.

'Madam,' the A.C.P. answered, with not a little sharpness now, 'I am a fully trained police officer, as also is Inspector Ghote here. Kindly do not think that we do not know what evidences are to be found on a body that has drowned. Now, let me ask you this: did that Medical Officer's report from Vigatpore state there was no observed blueness of the nails? Or did it simply fail to mention such?'

And the bhabhi, for all her former fearlessness, quailed.

'It did not mention,' she murmured. 'But that must be meaning there was no such sign present.'

'Not at all, madam, not at all. Are you thinking that a medical officer in such a mofussil place is any sort of a genius fellow? It is lucky he was even mentioning other signs of drowning. Did he state, yes or no, that there was water in the lungs and internal cavities?'

Ghote waited for the answer. Dreading it. But again the bhabhi was honest.

'Yes,' she said dispiritedly. 'He was stating. In an altogether text-book manner. Some evidence of water, he was saying.'

Ghote rejoiced. What luck that this medico was a fellow gripped entirely by the text-books. Evidently he must have found water in the internal cavities and, because it was written down that water also would get into the lungs, he had stated that it had been there. But, as the A.C.P. had said, it was unlikely that a medical officer anywhere as out-of-the-way as Vigatpore would be a genius fellow.

'Well, it is just as I thought,' the A.C.P. was saying, in an encouraging tone as he got up from behind his desk. 'I am glad, madam, that we have been able to set your doubts and those of your husband at rest. And may I also add my sincere condolences?'

Slowly the bhabhi rose from her chair. The look of defeat was plain to see on her face.

Ghote felt sorry for her. She had fought a good fight, and, little though she had known it, right had after all been on her side. Desai had not drowned. But if that had been proved, what consequences there might have been for Tiger Kelkar. And himself.

Then almost at the door the bhabhi turned and confronted the A.C.P. once more.

'No,' she said loudly. 'No, I still do not believe that Subhash could have drowned. I have seen his swimming powers with my own eyes.'

'But, madam –'

'No, Mr Assistant Commissioner, if you will not grant us full inquiry, one of my batch-mates at college is now an investigative reporter for *Sunday Observer*. She would bring everything into open.'

'But – But –'

Ghote had never seen the A.C.P. at such a loss. He wished he himself was not present.

'But, madam,' the A.C.P. brought out at last, 'kindly do not be thinking that I have in any way rejected a police inquiry. Such an inquiry, indeed, is what we would expect to hold in the circumstances. That I can promise.'

The bhabhi stood for a moment at the door, fierce and proud in her bright red sari.

'Very well, Mr Assistant Commissioner,' she said, 'we shall expect to hear what progress is made.'

And she left.

The A.C.P. coughed.

'Let that be a lesson to you, Ghote,' he said, 'if at any time you rise to senior rank. Too much importance can never be placed on good relations with the public.'

'No, sir,' Ghote said.

He found himself torn in the days that followed between a hope that the A.C.P. had merely been offering something sweet to appease the ferocious young woman who had been confronting him and a fear that an inquiry would be ordered and that it would somehow uncover the stratagems even of Tiger Kelkar.

And there was, too, deep-down a feeling, which he did his best to quell, that he wanted any investigation which Desai's bhabhi had won for herself to succeed. To do what it ought to do, reveal the truth.

So it was with not entirely unmixed feelings, one day some three weeks later, that he heard that Inspector Sawant had been handed the job of conducting an inquiry into Desai's death and that he wanted to talk to him.

Sawant was a hard-working, conscientious fellow, but he was not the sort of pushing investigator that in his day Tiger had been. He would look at all the facts that came before him and he would draw the logical conclusions that were there to be made from them. But no more.

So the chances were high that what he and Tiger had put there to be discovered would be brought to light, and the conclusion they had put there to be drawn would once more be arrived at.

He felt little anxiety, then, over the interview with Sawant, and had no difficulty in producing the few necessary evasions and the few necessary lies. He even managed to drop a hint about Desai's mania for betting while not, he felt, pitching it too strong.

'Thank you, Ghote,' Sawant said at the end. 'I have yet to go to Vigatpore, of course, but I do not think I would need to trouble you again. I have about as much chance, after all, of finding there was anything amiss as a fakir has of solving a crime by opening a page of the Koran at rupees ten a time.'

And that was that.

Once more he was able to push the events of the night of June 24 into the back of his mind. He could not quite blot them out as completely as before. He caught himself occasionally worrying over whether poor, saluting Shinde would stick to the story he had given him if he was questioned, and at other times he wondered whether the bet business had been really too weak. But mostly he was able to exclude all thoughts of Vigatpore from his head for two or three days at a time.

It was only his catching sight, one day towards the end of May, of Inspector Sawant's burly form going out of the Headquarters' gate that gave him one final jab of anxiety.

He set off after him at a run and succeeded in catching him by the arm as he was waiting halfway across the traffic jostle of D. N. Road on the pocket of safety formed by the jutting stones of the twin parallel road dividers.

'Sawantji,' he said, 'how are you?'

'Fine. Fine, Ghote bhai. Just off to Vigatpore, one last time, thank goodness.'

'Oh, yes? All gone okay, has it?'

'Yes, yes. Nothing other than what it seemed, of course. Only one last thing remaining. The fellow's clothes had never come to light. It is possible, I have been thinking, that he would have had in his pocket some note of any bet he had made about swimming Lake Helena in a monsoon storm, and I would like to be able to state who he had made it with. Tidying up, you know.'

'Oh, yes,' Ghote answered, able to assume a proper carelessness because that was exactly what he felt. 'Well, good luck, bhai. I won't keep you.'

What in fact had he done with Desai's clothes? he asked himself almost idly. In the final confusion of that terrible night he had disposed of them somehow. But where? He had completely forgotten now.

'Goodbye then,' Sawant said hurriedly. 'I am a little late for train.'

'Right then. Goodbye.'

But just at that moment a new surge of traffic came sweeping round from Lokmanya Tilak Road and Sawant was unable to make his plunge for the far side. He turned to Ghote again with a shrug.

'By the way,' he said, 'I was hearing only good reports of your time in Vigatpore. You were setting right a lot that Inspector Khan, who is nothing but a hopeless slacker, had let go wrong.'

Ghote felt a surge of pleasure.

'Oh, well,' he said, 'I was doing my level best only. But I was not there too long, you know. Some things still in a hell of a mess. Did you see inside the Muddamal Room?'

And the moment the words were out of his mouth he was appalled by what he had said. Of course. That was where he had stuffed away that damn blood-stained jacket. In the Muddamal Room. Tucked behind a confiscated public-address loudspeaker – he could see it now – and easy enough to find if anyone took the trouble to look.

'Muddamal Room,' Sawant said. 'Do you know I have never looked in there, and I even thought at one time it was possible the fellow had stripped to undershorts in the station itself. With the rain there was that night it would have been quite a sensible thing to do.'

'Yes,' Ghote said, deep in despondency.

He looked down at the rough stones of the road divider at his feet.

'But Desai was not at all sensible,' he said desperately.

Inspector Sawant, however, had seen his chance and had darted across the road in front of a boldly decorated truck taking vegetables round to the back of Crawford Market.

61

7

Ghote stood where he was amid the tangy metallic fumes of the jockeying, jostling traffic of D. N. Road as the full bitterness of the situation swamped through his mind. How could he have been such a fool? When Sawant had said plainly that his inquiries had produced nothing, to go and throw out such a clue to the beginning of it all. How could he have failed to remember where he had put that jacket of Desai's with the blood clear on its collar? But he had. In his overwhelming need to put behind him everything coming after the moment of Tiger's rage he had succeeded only too well in blotting out that one vital detail.

Or had some inner force he was quite unaware of pushed up into daylight the devastating truth at just the worst possible moment?

Because it was almost certain now that Sawant, who was nothing if not methodical, would at once ask himself why Desai's uniform was bloodstained. And then the end of the long thread leading to the truth would be in his hand.

All that he himself and Tiger had done to conceal that single rage-provoked error would be in terrible danger of being brought to ruin.

Tiger.

taken to wandering into headquarters to chat
willing to spare him time.

you these days then?' Ghote asked, resigning
enty minutes or more of placid chit-chat.

well. Pretty well, considering. I keep busy, you
g about, looking for things gone astray. Times
n bad to worse, you know. Bad to worse. You've
Tiger Kelkar?'

a jab of ice enter him. Tiger. What could there
hear about Tiger?

instants he remained incapable of speaking,
replying in any reasonable off-hand way to
ut piece of gossip.

managed at last. 'No. What to hear?'

you have heard nothing?' D'Sa asked, provok-
ow an uprush of irritation that made him want
is chair, seize the old fool by the shoulders and
he rattled.

ok him some moments to get out a decently

m hearing nothing. What news is it?'

lking to Commissioner Sahib,' D'Sa answered
. 'Always has a few minutes for an old officer,
r Sahib. A real gentleman.'

was he telling?' Ghote could hardly keep the
voice.

Tiger has shot himself,' D'Sa replied com-
w out his brains yesterday afternoon. Commis-
wouldn't tell me just why. But there is some
lal, believe you me.'

ow's eyes gleamed joyfully.

sat there unable to utter, unable to think,

ote read the Commissioner's memo for the
, eighth time.

Abruptly it came to him that what he had done was to put Tiger in peril once more. And worse peril than he had been in at the moment he had killed Desai. There was no hope of him, even from Pune, being able to get to Vigatpore ahead of Sawant, not if Sawant was leaving Bombay in a few minutes' time. So the damning evidence was bound to come to light. Blood on the uniform of the supposedly drowned man. That uniform hidden, and hidden in the police station. And when had the station been all but deserted? Only when he himself and the A.D.I.G., working late on his Inspection, had been alone there.

And he did not even know if Tiger had succeeded in establishing his own scrap of alibi by faking the time he had returned to the Inspection Bungalow.

The least he could do now was to give him warning.

Leadenly he turned, waited for the traffic to clear between himself and the pavement outside Headquarters with its row of squatting newspaper sellers up against the wall and made his way across.

Leadenly he tramped to his office. How was he to break the news? Tiger would scorch him with his anger for the stupidity of the mistake he had made. But tell him of it he must. He owed him that. To learn that their ruse, seemingly hidden by now in the wrappings of time, had so unexpectedly risen to light: that chance at least he must give to Tiger.

And with it the possibility, slim to nothingness though it must be, of his hitting on some way of accounting for that blood on the jacket of the supposedly drowned man.

But Tiger's fury would be horrible.

Leadenly he sat himself down at his desk and picked up the telephone to put a call through to Pune. He would have to be guarded on an open line. But Tiger would understand quickly enough. And react.

He had more than a little difficulty in getting to speak to a figure as senior as A.D.I.G. Kelkar. But he persisted, tempted though he was more than once to put down the receiver and give up, escaping the wrath that would await him.

'Ghote?'

The voice at the other end of the line, distorted and buzz-blurred though it was, was unmistakable.

'Yes, sir. It is me. Sir, I have some news which I am thinking you –'

He came to a dead halt. Somewhere here at headquarters or there at Pune someone might be listening in.

'Sir, some news I am thinking you would like to hear.'

'Yes, Inspector?' the voice crackled.

'Sir, owing to something I regret for stating to a third party without due and proper caution, sir, they are about to –'

Again he came to a stop.

He ought to have spent time framing a properly concealed message.

'Speak up, man. I'm not sitting in my seat just waiting to hear what you see fit to tell me.'

The whip-crack he had feared. But there would be worse, far, far worse, soon.

'No, sir. No. Sir, it is the jacket. The one with – with something on it, sir. It is about to be discovered. In two-three hours only.'

'Discovered? Where, man, where?'

'In the Muddamal Room at the –'

'All right, Inspector,' Tiger cut in, his voice not raised in anger but incisive as ever. 'That was where you put it, was it? Put it and the rest?'

'Yes, sir, I –'

'Where are you speaking from, Inspector?'

'Bombay, sir.'

'I see. Then no chance of you getting there first. Or of myself, come to that.'

'No, sir. I am most sorry, sir, but that night –'

'That will do, Inspector.'

The shortest of pauses. A[...] voice again, sharp and swif[...] ordinarily – without the least [...]

'Thank you for keeping me [...] And the line went dead.

Ghote sat there, the uppe[...] trembling in the aftermath of [...]

Had he managed to tell Ti[...] he had. There was only really [...] unforgivable thing: that he [...] bloodstained jacket was the[...] Vigatpore. To be found wh[...] mean one thing only, that a d[...] in the station, that the woun[...] inflicted in the lake, that he [...] for that absurd swim, but ha[...] And at a time when only [...] station building.

Tiger could easily enou[...] that. Tiger would work it [...] himself.

But what would Tiger d[...] What Tiger did Ghote le[...]

Over the bat-wing door[...] head and shoulders of old [...]

'Ah, Ghote. How are th[...] am glad to see.'

He pushed open the do[...] down with a long puff of a[...]

'Damned hot,' he grum[...] late this year. When you [...]

Ghote suppressed a ri[...] boy must find it hard a[...] routine work, in which [...] particular to do. He had [...] that many retired officer[...]

months,[...]
with any[...]

'How [...]
himself [...]

'Oh, p[...]
know. W[...]
are going [...]
heard ab[...]

Ghote [...]
be alread[...]

For sev[...]
incapable[...]
D'Sa's he[...]

'Tiger?'[...]

'You m[...]
ing in Gho[...]
to leap fro[...]
shake him [...]

Again it[...]
polite reply[...]

'No. No, [...]

'I was u[...]
painstaking[...]
Commissio[...]

'But wha[...]
rage out of [...]

'Why, th[...]
fortably. 'B[...]
sioner Sahi[...]
sort of a sca[...]

The old fe[...]
And Gho[...]
unable to fee[...]

Inspector G[...]
sixth, seventh[...]

From the Commissioner of Police, Bombay
To: Inspector G. V. Ghote

I have considered certain events alleged to have occurred at Vigatpore P.S. on the night of June 24/25 last year and I must request a full account of your part therein. I require to have the aforesaid account before me by 0900 hours on Monday, June 4.

What could he say? What could he answer?

One thing was clear. It had been becoming more and more so since he had heard that Tiger had shot himself: whatever note or confession he had left behind had not mentioned his own part in the events of that terrible night. Otherwise he would have received, not a request like the one staring him in the face at this moment, but a visit from a senior officer with an arrest warrant.

Tiger had too much of loyalty to have betrayed him. That was certain.

No, the reason this memo was lying on his desk was that there must have been, of course, an investigation already. As soon as the Inspector-General had read Tiger's last letter he would have ordered an inquiry. Sent some officer from Vigilance Branch at Pune to check up on each and every detail of what Tiger had written. Tiger must certainly have said that he had taken the body to Lake Helena on his own, and that in itself was not very likely. In fact the two of them together had had enough difficulty getting it there. Perhaps already some kind of experiment with a dummy and a police bicycle had been carried out. And if as a result the officer making this new investigation – coming from Vigilance he would be a lot sharper than old Sawant – suspected a second person must be involved, his own position was bound to have come under scrutiny. Then, at the least the investigator would have discovered from questioning the men sent off duty that night that he himself had been left eventually alone in the building with Tiger.

But no one else, surely, had witnessed any of the incidents

of that night, except only Shivram Patel's servant admitting him to the house at the end of it all. And even then the fellow had accepted without any protest his lie about the time. So there was nothing for even the keenest investigator to find. Whatever suspicions there might be, there was nothing that could be proved.

He was at liberty then to say whatever he wished in answer to the Commissioner.

Could he, if he wanted, say exactly what had occurred? From start to finish? From that absurd, unnecessary moment when he had ordered Desai to take the F.I.R. book in to the A.D.I.G. right on to the moment when he himself had thrust the bundle of Desai's clothes to the back of the shelf in the Muddamal Room behind the loudspeaker?

Could he? Should he?

Ever since he had heard of Tiger's death, knowing that sooner or later he was bound to get this request from the Commissioner, he had asked himself time and again these questions. And had not been able to find an answer.

Somehow, too, he had been unable to confide in anybody. Not even Protima back at home, although she had questioned him and questioned him sharply in that way of hers more than once about his lack of appetite, his long lying awake at night. But, for all that he loved her as his wife, for all that he trusted her, he had not felt able to unburden himself to her of his secret. It was too fast entwined among all that in his innermost being he believed in for him to be able to pull it out, whole and writhing, and present it, bare, even to the wife of his bosom, even to his Sita to his Rama, one he knew would make any sacrifice for him, just as he was.

Much, much less had he felt he could talk to any one of his colleagues however much, understanding the full circumstances of his position, they might have been able to give him good advice.

He had known he was clinging to an altogether false hope, but until he had actually seen the memo with his own eyes he had still felt dimly that what had happened had not properly happened.

But now he had seen the memo. Its words were there staring him in the face.

A full account of your part therein.

By Monday morning.

At least then he had a day to think it all over again. One day.

He felt a qualm of sickness.

Before Monday morning he would have had to have decided something that might mean the whole course of his life would be altered. And not only of his life, of Protima's and of Ved's, too. Of Ved's, with all his promise.

But if in answer to the Commissioner he was to state the full facts that had led to that moment of plunging commitment in Vigatpore, then he would be brought up in no time at all before a Board of Inquiry, and at it he would have no alternative but to recapitulate his confession. And then . . . Then, almost certainly, having admitted to a crime as grave as concealing the evidence of a culpable homicide, he would be necked out of the police. Necked out of his life as it was.

What would he do after that? He might be able to get some sort of work, though with graduate unemployment running as high as it was, youngsters just out of college applying for a mere clerk's job by the hundred, he might not even get that. And Protima would suffer, and Ved. Ved would suffer worse. He might have to go out at once and earn what he could, earn something to put a bite of food in their mouths. So no more progress. All bright hopes tumbled into the dust, tossed into the drain to rot and be swirled away. No Police Commissioner Ved Ghote. No police officer post even. But life as a coolie. Or a handcart walla. Or a pavement vendor.

Unless he himself persisted with the lie he and Tiger had built up together on that terrible night. He had been happy then to do what he had done. It had been worth every twist of deceit, every agony he had endured, to keep Tiger, fierce, cleansing, scarifying Tiger, in the police service.

But Tiger was no more in the police service. Tiger was dead. And all that the lie and the deceit would do now was to keep him himself, Tiger's pale shadow, as a police officer.

Was he worth it? Was he, pale though he was, enough of Tiger's shadow to justify that lie? To justify cheating that poor, full-of-guts bhabhi of Desai's? To justify living the rest of his life protected by a monstrous lie?

And there was one day now only to decide. One day.

8

Ghote stood, rooted in indecision, beside his scooter a good hour earlier than his usual time of departure for home on a Saturday. He was unable to make up his mind to leave even though he had tidied away all the papers on his desk and left himself nothing to do.

He felt gripped in every way by his inability to decide what answer to give to the Commissioner.

At last, glimpsing a fellow officer over on the far side of the compound and thinking he might come across to chat, he hurriedly got astride his machine and kicked it into spluttering life. But even when he arrived home after phut-phutting his way through the still busy working city he still could not bring himself to tear loose the intertwined secret deep within him.

He ate even less than he had in the past few days of the food, the meal cooked just to his taste, that Protima had prepared. And then he sat, sat in his customary chair, that mark of stability, of a future stretching out, and did nothing and said nothing.

More than once Protima asked him questions, more and more trivial questions needing less and less of an answer and put with ever-increasing quick sharpness. And each time he grunted out the barest of answers. Ved, sensing that something had gone much astray, after one application for money to buy a paper cone of spicy chana had met with blank silence, took himself off idly kicking at imaginary stones to play with his friends. He came back at the promised hour, but Ghote, who liked nothing better than to offer him praise, again could not bring himself to utter a word.

Ved mooched off to bed, and a little later, much before his usual time, Ghote grunted out that he was sleepy too.

But, of course, in bed he lay sleepless, stiff on his back, hands underneath his head, uncomfortably sweating, and soon aware that in the other cot Protima, too, was not asleep.

At last there came the query in the hot darkness.

'Are you awake?'

He knew that this was the moment he had been really waiting for, wanting even. But still he could not wrench out that tangle of fears and feelings inside him.

'I know you are awake. Why is it you cannot sleep? What are you worrying?'

'It is nothing.'

'No. I know it is something. What it is? What?'

He lay there silent still, a sort of smouldering resentment filling him, against Protima for no reason, against life because he was victim of such a conspiracy of circumstances.

Protima slipped out of bed and came across. She sat on the side of his cot.

'Please,' she said.

He felt all the depth of the plea, a depth the greater for Protima, customarily a jetting fount of words, having confined it to that single, heart-tugging syllable. But the very pull of it seemed to increase in his breast the determination not to speak.

Not to have to speak. He lay thickly wishing for some intervention from above, from anywhere, that would provide an answer without him ever having to drag from within himself the words, the explanation, that must be there, absolutely unwilling though he was to examine what they were.

In the hot silence Protima sat on the end of his cot without another sound.

He began then, perversely, to wish she would speak.

She has only once to ask, he said to himself. That is all. If she would speak one word only. But she will not. And if she can be so bloody obstinate, at a time like this, I will be also.

He knew he was being ridiculous. Unfair and ridiculous. But he began to take a positive malign pleasure in that unfairness.

Then in the dark he heard Protima sob. A single, checked, quickly suppressed sob.

And at last the twice-locked floodgates burst open.

'I have done something terrible, terrible.'

So he told her everything, from the arrival of Tiger Kelkar on his Inspection to the moment when the news that Tiger had shot himself had so abruptly come to his ears, with all too soon afterwards the arrival of the Commissioner's memo.

She said nothing for two or three long stifling minutes. Then she spoke.

'And what you will say in your answer that you must give?'

'I do not know. The truth, perhaps. All that I have just only told you.'

'And what will happen then?'

'There would be an Inquiry by the Commissioner. There will be one, whatever I am saying.'

'And?'

'Oh, I do not know. Yes, I do. I have thought about it. There are many things they could do to me, when they know what I have done. I could receive censure only. But that is not likely after what I did, after what Kelkar Sahib and I did. Or I could have promotion withheld. But if it was only that . . . Or, I suppose, they could say that my actions had caused expenditure of police time, and deduction from pay was in order. Or there is reduction to a lower stage in the pay time-scale for a period to be specified. Or, and this is the least that is likely, reduction in rank.'

'To constable?'

'No, no. They are not able to do that. Reduction in rank is always at most to that at which service was entered.'

'So you would become sub-inspector once more?'

'Yes. But it might not be only that. There is compulsory retirement. And . . .'

'Yes? What else?'

'Dismissal. Perhaps also in that case a charge under Section 201, causing disappearance of evidence of an offence committed or giving false information touching it so as to screen an offender.'

Protima sat silent then on the side of the bed. It seemed to Ghote that he could sense the chill desolateness that was entering her. He wanted to say something that would push it away. But what was there he could say? The truth was there between them, just as his long, obstinate silence had been earlier. If the full extent of what he had done that night in Vigatpore came out before an Inquiry, then certainly one of the worst of the alternatives he had told her of would be visited upon him.

Dismissal.

The end of his life as he had known it, as he had expected to know it till the finish of his working days and beyond.

And had not Tiger Kelkar seen just such an end facing him? And taken his way out?

He knew, lying there in the stifling darkness of the pre-monsoon night, that Tiger's way was not for him. Perhaps he lacked the courage. Perhaps he simply did not feel himself to be spewing up such a fiery lava-stream of self-anger. Perhaps he was too aware of how he would be deserting Protima and Ved, fruit of their union.

But, if Tiger's way was barred to him, what other was there?

He found his mind all grey blankness.

'But, if supposing . . .' Protima said at last, her voice small and without hope in the dark.

'If supposing I am dismissed?'

'Yes.'

He uttered a sigh, a sigh that had more than a little of tears in it.

'I do not know,' he said finally. 'What else than police work am I fit for? It is all I have ever wanted to do. It is all I have ever done. It is all I have ever hoped to do.'

'Yes.'

An acknowledgement.

He felt a spasm of ridiculously petty irritation.

'What good would I be as a security officer?' he broke out. 'Oh, I could do that job all right, but what of satisfaction would be there? And in any case I do not think I would be getting. Who is going to want a dismissed fellow? Even old D'Sa, you know, thirty-five years unblemished service, he could not get such a post.'

'But then . . . Then how would we make our both ends meet?'

'I do not know. I do not know. There would be some way, I suppose. Other people keep from starving to death. We should do the same. But . . .'

He lay there in silence again, bitter silence. Near the foot of the bed he could feel waves of encouragement emanating from Protima, waves of sympathy, of hope. But what good were they in face of the future that inevitably, it seemed, awaited him?

'It is not as if I have not been a good officer,' he flared out suddenly. 'Have I taken bribes? You have complained even that we never had "income from above". Have I aided and abetted criminal elements? Have I toadied and treated reverently superior officers? No, I have never so much as held open one car door to them. Have I had suspects beaten up even? Had them hung by the arms and cane-hit till they talked? Did I buy my posting to the C.I.D.? And now I am to lose everything after I have sweated every ounce of my blood, and all because of one terrible night only.'

Protima made no answer to this tirade. But when at last she did speak what she said came at Ghote like a flung bucket of cold water.

'Then there is one thing to do only. You must give out a lie.'

Her voice in the dark was calm and resolved.

'But – But – But I cannot do that. Oh, cover up for a fellow officer when it would not make much of difference, that I could do. That was what I was doing for Tiger Kelkar. That was all I was doing. But to lie for myself now that he has gone. To lie not just only to someone who is asking something, but to lie and lie before an Inquiry. No, I cannot do it.'

'But you must. If you do not you would not have your work and we shall be ground down to beggars also. You, I myself, Ved. To beggars.'

Ghote lay there in the darkness. Protima, a vague outline against the lesser darkness of the window behind her, was no longer that softly emanating presence, wafting towards him sympathy, hope. Useless hope and ineffectual sympathy, but hope nevertheless. Now she was the tower of a fort looking down on an enemy country. Refusing passage.

The minutes passed.

He felt that he must say something more. But he was not going to give in. He had told her what was in the core of his heart, and there it was.

At last he found a few words.

'Tomorrow. Tomorrow we would talk again. Perhaps I shall be able to sleep now . . . You must sleep also.'

'Tomorrow,' Protima answered, rising silently from the cot. 'But you must tell that lie. I know it.'

He did sleep, but not much and not for a long time after Protima had gone back to her own bed. And when morning came he knew he was not going to keep his half-promise of talking again.

He knew still, grittily and snarlingly, that he did not want to put himself in a position to be persuaded or cajoled or bribed or bullied into changing his mind. He had not been ready, when it had come down to it, to lie his way out of the black trouble he had got himself into. And now, in the light of day, he was prepared to do it still less.

So, as soon as he decently could, he announced that he was going for a walk. Taking a Sunday morning stroll had never been a custom with him, but Protima made no comment when he said he was going and she even, with a quick flash of fire, silenced young Ved when he seemed inclined to question this departure from the normal.

He tramped out – the pavements seemed hardly to have lost the stored heat of the sultry day before – and set off in the first direction that occurred to him.

He knew that what he ought to be doing was thinking out precisely what he should say in the memo he had to have on the Commissioner's desk by 0900 hours next morning. But he knew that he was going to do no such thing. He was too full of a glowering determination to have done with the whole business, to come out with the entire truth about that appalling, muddled night and let what would happen then happen.

So he marched grimly along scarcely seeing any of the city's Sunday morning sights, the squatting man holding an arm high to have the hair shaved from under it by a pavement barber, boys playing cricket in a side lane happily free of passers-by, the card in the window of a television and radio shop reading loftily *Forgiveness is Better Than Revenge* – Yes, he thought briefly, but is weakness better than anger? – a pair of khaki-clad municipal cleaners, baskets on heads, drifting along picking up rubbish from the gutter, a madman holding in one hand a hole-pocked umbrella against the sun and with the other furiously menacing unseen enemies.

Somewhere on his determined, black-thoughted tramp he realised that a cloud had darkened the sun and looked up.

Yes, dark enough as a cloud but nowhere near to being filled with the monsoon rain that would tumble out in a delicious cooling downpour.

He wondered then if Protima had made all her monsoon preparations. She ought to have put silica gel pouches in his shoes. At an Inquiry he would have to wear uniform, probably his review uniform, and what if the shoes were green with mould? But gels cost three rupees each, and in a month or two, perhaps less, he might have no income at all.

His eye was caught by a huddle of street boys beside the kerb, very much intent on whatever it was they were doing, arguing hotly among themselves, oblivious of anyone near.

And abruptly he knew what it was they were busy about. They were blocking a drain so that, when the monsoon did come, the torrential rainwater would not be able to gurgle away and there would be a deep flood – Yes, the road dipped just here – and cars that had come to a stop could be pushed to dry land by boys who happened to be there, and who would be rewarded.

It happened every monsoon.

Purposefully he set off towards the group. He could think of no particular section of the Indian Penal Code to hammer down on to their trifling crime. But crime it was and he was a police officer.

He came to a dead halt some two or three paces from the unnoticing huddle. Yes, he was a police officer now, but for how long was he going to go on being one? In a few weeks at the most he would be no more than an ordinary citizen, no longer specifically charged with upholding the law, keeping the peace, righting wrong, protecting the innocent.

He stood looking unseeingly now at the jabbering conspiracy of urchins, his lips pursed.

Then he turned slowly, and slowly made his way home. He knew that Protima would at once ask him what he intended to do, as if the purpose of his walk could only have been to think out his position. But nevertheless he went home.

And Protima, at once, pulled him into the little window-less kitchen so as to be able to talk out of sight of Ved, engrossed in a paperback *Sunny Gavaskar, Cricket Hero*. In her eagerness she did not even allow him time to kick the chappals off his feet before entering the little room. And there she looked him straight in the eye and fired out one short question.

'Well, you have decided to lie as much as you must?'

'No,' he said.

But he knew that he had failed to put into that single syllable all the force he would have done the night before. And Protima detected instantly the undertone of doubt.

'How can I persuade?' she said, almost with tears. 'Why you will not see reason? It is your whole life you would be saving. It is our livelihood also.'

'But how can I lie and lie?' he asked, and again knew he had been less adamant than he should have been.

She darted him a glance then which, he knew, would at any other time have been the prelude to an outburst of within-the-family fury. But now she was forcing that back. The situation was too serious for everyday ways.

'Please, my husband,' she said, 'if you will not listen to me, will you do one thing for me?'

He scented a trap. But she had earned an answer.

'What thing?'

'Would you come with me to the temple, to Pandit Balkrishan? He would give you a good advice.'

A flame of revolt shot up in him.

'No. No. You know I am never having anything to do with those priest fellows.'

'Yes, well I am knowing. But till now you have never been on the edge of being no longer a police officer.'

Ghote felt the words as a thumping blow. They had done no more than put before him what he had looked at in his mind a hundred times in the last few days, the very thought that had sent him turning on his heels as he had advanced upon the urchin wrongdoers at the road drain. But somehow, coming from his wife's own lips, they seemed to have a force that was redoubled. More than redoubled, was twenty, fifty times more affecting.

But to go to Protima's latest hero-worshipped pandit? The man whose praises he had had to hear sung for the past year or more. And had had difficulty keeping his mouth shut each time. To go to that fellow for wisdom: it would be a double betrayal. It would be betraying his long-held convictions about the mumbo-jumbo of religion, and it would be admitting the possibility of abandoning his brick-built determination not to stand before the Commissioner's Inquiry and lie.

'But – But –' he said, searching more to find a stance he could justify than for words of answer.

Protima stood facing him in the little kitchen, its air still tangily smoky from the puris she had fried for breakfast. In the confined space she was of necessity almost close up against him. He could not avoid her gaze, direct as an upwards dagger thrust.

'My husband, I have not often begged of you in the years of our marriage, and I would not beg for myself. But it is for you, you yourself, that I am begging. Come and hear what Panditji has to tell.'

'Oh, yes then, yes, yes, yes,' he shouted, and turned and marched out again, out of the kitchen, out to the street.

But he knew that he would return in time to be led like a goat about to be sacrificed to visit that afternoon Pandit Balkrishan.

Sure enough, late afternoon found him with Protima in one of her best saris making his way, silent and rebelliously sulky within, up the steps of the narrow crowded path leading to the Banganga Tank on the heights of Walkeshwar and to the temple by its waters where Pandit Balkrishan was

80

a priest. At another time he might have enjoyed the bright and busy scene: a pair of men pounding green coriander and purplish onions to prepare masala, the dark open interior of a shop, its shelves lined with metal bowls heaped high with spices and condiments, rich brown, pure white, vibrant yellow, a woman leading a bony cow on a rope with grass to sell by the handful to anyone wishing to gain merit by feeding the slowly chewing animal. But all he could think of now was how much he hated the trappings and tarnishings of religion and how in a few minutes he was to be plunged into the middle of them for the first time in years.

Soon they came to the big, green-watered expanse of the Tank, that holiest of places, held to be equal to Mother Ganges, shaded at its sides by delicate light green pipal trees, looked down upon by old heaped-high buildings, its steps crumbling but thronged with half-naked or wet sari-clinging pilgrims all among the chickens scratching and pecking in the sun, with other worshippers by the score in the water, dipping and praying.

Now Protima was leading him past the chief temple with the polished black stone Nandi bull outside and pilgrims entering in a constant stream, tugging each one at the cord of the bell over their heads as they passed. And then they were at the temple where Pandit Balkrishan was a pujari.

He was conducting worship as they entered, a big shaven-headed man with his one remaining long tuft dangling down on massive fleshy pale brown shoulders and the pair of heavy spectacles he wore slipping off the tops of his ears as he ducked and sang.

But it was what he was singing that struck at Ghote like a snake rearing up from deep unsuspected darkness. *Jai Jagdish Hare*. It was the song of prayer he remembered from the days when his mother had taken him with her to the village temple when he was too young even to have dreamt of the rebellion of later years. He could feel now, suddenly, the texture of her sari as his hand had clutched its corner. And he could hear again the pujari of that small, ill-kept temple of long ago. His son, Ram, had been his own best friend, a boy marked out by the violence of his fits of temper, which perhaps accounted for his father's seldom abated air of bitterness. But bitterness did not affect him when he sang the praises of the god.

That voice, pure and love-filled, came into his ears again now. The old cranky pujari in the little, sweat-smelling, dirty temple put Pandit Balkrishan, careful, melodious and oozing contentment, right out of count. And the memory brought back a longing for the days that had been simple.

But those days were no more.

Ten minutes later he was sitting cross-legged on the floor of Pandit Balkrishan's room at the rear of the temple. The pandit, naked above the waist but for the white line of his sacred thread running across almost pendulous breasts and down to a rounded stomach, its feathering of hair just catching the light, faced him, one elbow resting on the bedroll behind him.

Any hopes of simply talking about any subject at all bar what was most in his mind and pretending at the end to take the fellow's blessing were quickly and thoroughly crushed by Protima. With many a 'Panditji' she simply explained the full extent of his dilemma.

Ghote, listening to the recital of his woes that he had poured out only the night before in the privacy and intimacy of their bedroom, felt a new resentment spring up in him.

'Yes, beta,' the pujari said, turning to Ghote when Protima had finished, 'you do well to come to me. What for is a pandit but to show how the teachings of religion help the difficulties of life?'

Ghote's barely suppressed distaste rose up at once. Why should this fellow, hardly older than himself despite his girth and air of contented authority, why should he call him *beta*? He was not the man's child. They were equals. Or should be.

'I have come because my wife was insisting,' he said, scarcely keeping the rage out of his voice.

'Yes, it is fine to have the hopes and the prayers of a good Hindu wife when times are troublesome.'

'They are not so much of troublesome.'

'No, beta? What your good wife was telling makes me think you are in great trouble. Very great trouble.'

'Well, I will think what I must do before long.'

Behind the heavy hornrims on the pandit's fleshy curving nose his eyes glinted acutely.

'But you have not got long to think. By nine pip emma tomorrow you must give your answer, isn't it?'

Ghote felt a new resentment. Why should this priest, this fellow who was meant to be unworldly if anyone was, have seized so accurately on the details of his predicament?

'Well, by that time I will have thought,' he said.

'And what will be the answer you give? Will you tell all the truth of this terrible-terrible situation you have put yourself into? Or will you find this is a time when the truth that floats on the surface must give way to the truth under the water?'

Hypocrite, Ghote exploded internally. Just like all temple-wallas. Hypocrite. Hypocrite. Hypocrite.

'Well, beta, which answer will you give?'

'I do not know.'

Why, why, had he said that? He did know. He had known from the moment Protima had forced him to consider the question, there in the darkness of their room. He was not going to lie. Not to save himself. So why had he told this smooth-bellied creature in front of him that he did not know what answer to give?

Was it because he did not, in fact, know?

'Then let me repeat to you a verse of the Geeta.'

At once the pujari launched into a high singsong recitation.

'Do you follow that?' he asked, a look of satisfaction on his ample face at the mellifluousness he had brought to the quotation.

'No,' Ghote answered, such Sanskrit as he had half-mastered forgotten long ago.

'Then I will tell it to you in chaste Marathi. *From anger comes bewilderment, from bewilderment wandering of the mind, from wandering of the mind destruction of the soul; once the soul is destroyed the man is lost.* And you are lost in anger, beta, isn't it?'

Ghote sat silent.

Opposite him, rounded and heavy as a sack of grain, Pandit Balkrishan was equally silent.

At last Ghote spoke.

'But what to blame if I am angry?' he said. 'Fate has played me one bitch of a trick, no? All I was doing was helping a senior officer, a man I am altogether admiring, when by some bad chance a terrible thing had happened to him. And now I am staring in the face the end of everything I have always wanted to do.'

'Yes,' said Pandit Balkrishan, 'now you begin to see.'

'See? What see?'

'What your life is. What is your karma for this time of yours in the world. To see that. Do you remember in the Mahabharata what advice Mareecha was giving to Ravana when he did not wish to fight against his brother?'

Ghote looked at the floor between his knees.

'Not altogether,' he answered.

'Well then, I will quote it to you. He was saying: *You are a warrior. The exercise of valour is your proper task. What are your gifts worth if you let them go unused?*'

He gave Ghote a wide-grinning, inquiring smile.

'Are you going to go on trying to use those gifts which you have?' he said.

'Yes,' said Inspector Ghote.

9

Sir, Most respectfully it is submitted as under:

On the night of June 24/25 last I, as in-charge, temporary, at Vigatpore P.S., left duty at approximately 2330 hours when I had ascertained that A.D.I.G. Kelkar, conducting the Inspection then proceeding, no longer required my presence. In consequence I am not able to make any comment of my own knowledge on events that occurred later that night.

G. V. Ghote, Inspector

By noon on Monday, June 4, Ghote had been notified in answer to his memo that he was to appear before a Commissioner's Inquiry, his explanation of the Vigatpore events being in the opinion of the Commissioner 'not satisfactory.' In view of the seriousness of the matter he was suspended from duty 'as from this day's date'.

He had expected nothing else.

But – suspended. The notification still came as a blow. He had never remotely seen himself as doing anything in the course of his career that would bring about his suspension. He sat there at his desk – he must remember to take home his towel – and forced himself to think of the good side.

Withholding from the Commissioner what he could have

told him about Desai's death was something that he had decided, after much doubt, was what he ought to do. By his silence, and the direct lies that in due course would have to spring from it, he would be, unless something unimaginable occurred, ensuring his own future as a police officer. Not for his own benefit. Nor was it even so that his wife and son could live as they had always done, though this would be a bonus to his decision. It was in order that he should be able to go on doing what he did best, serving his fellow man by bringing the guilty to book, by seeing that the law was upheld.

He was serving the same cause, he thought, as when he had taken that first impulsive, fraught with consequences, rock-firm resolution to help Tiger. He had done that because he felt Tiger, sending his fire and vigour down through the ranks, was a force for good. Well, he himself in his lesser way would be that, too. He would, if he got through the time of trial that was awaiting him, take Tiger as his ever-to-be-followed model. He would be a better police officer for having told the lies that, all to soon, he must tell.

Yet the time of trial proved not to come as soon as, sitting there looking at the Commissioner's notification, he had seen it as beginning.

Evidence, he realised in the next few days, would still have to be gathered. That was something that could take weeks. A Presiding Officer for the Inquiry had to be found. He himself had to be given time in which to decide whether he wanted to be defended by a brother officer or to exercise his right to be represented legally, and in consequence face questioning not from the Presiding Officer himself but from a lawyer of equal eminence to his own – and perhaps even greater cross-examining skills.

So for an indefinite period he found himself at home with nothing to do. Day by day the pre-monsoon heat built up. And tension grew with it, in the city where there were frequent outbreaks of communal and domestic violence, and in his own home.

There was, about three weeks after his suspension had begun, the absurd incident of the umbrella. He had undertaken to go to Lohar Chawl in Protima's place to see if among all the hardware items the area specialised in, the plastic buckets in their bright towers, the electric toasters, the fan-shaped arrays of padlocks and furniture castors, the pyramids of crockery and glassware, he could find, cheap, an indoors clothesline so that this year when the rains came there would be less trouble getting garments dry.

Just as he had stepped out, the patchy clouds above had begun to produce a faint drizzle, as often happened before the monsoon itself started. He decided to go back for his umbrella. It would hardly be necessary, but finding it and taking it out would lengthen nicely this interruption in the idle monotony.

He spotted it in the first place he thought of as likely for it to have been put away at the end of the previous monsoon shortly after he had returned from Vigatpore. It was under the bed, and he groped for it, blew off some dust and set out once more.

But, when he came to open it, standing in the soft drizzle again and already beginning to feel stickily hot, something appeared to be wrong. It was a mechanical umbrella, useful in that it would fold compactly if he was using his scooter. Protima had given it to him in place of his former long one, which in fact he was proud of having kept intact, more or less, through four whole monsoons.

But now, wrestle with this one's catch as he might, nothing happened. The affair remained obstinately a small black tube.

Eventually, covered now in sweat, he attempted to prise the damn thing apart with his fingers. And at last it moved. Suddenly and with a loud ripping sound.

And there it was in his hands. Ruined.

Fury swept up in him, red, screaming fury, filling every corner of his mind, wildly blotting out everything.

'Damn, damn, damn,' he shouted, careless of what neighbour wives might hear. 'Damn, bloody, mother-raping thing.'

He hurled it on to the pavement and jumped up and down with both feet on the little heap of wreckage.

In a moment Protima appeared, curious to know what the disturbance was about.

'Blood, bloody stupid umbrella,' he yelled at her.

He knew he was rejecting her gift, and that this would hurt her. But in his pent-up rage, at last released after days and weeks of frustration, he was careless of any harm he might inflict on anyone.

'Where is my old umbrella?' he demanded. 'Where is an umbrella that is some damn bloody use?'

'It was of no use,' Protima answered with an air of calm that he knew she was deliberately putting on. 'There were holes all over. I was selling it long ago to the raddiwalla.'

'Then how do you expect me to go and get your damn clothesline in all this rain?' he stormed back at her.

'There is not much of rain and if you do not want to go you do not need.'

'Oh, well, I will go then. I will go. And if I am catching a cold and getting ill, then it is you who must take the blame.'

And off he marched.

He failed to find a clothesline at a sum he thought they could afford, now that his salary was 'held in arrears'. All the pavement umbrella sellers he saw, too, appeared to have hiked their prices in anticipation of the days of rain ahead. But nevertheless by the time he returned home, exhausted, his fury had blown itself out.

The days went slowly by. He saw few of his colleagues, and soon realised that most of them were avoiding the man with the dark shadow hanging over him. Even those who did go out of their way to greet him when he had occasion to go near Headquarters did so, he felt, too heartily.

How among such friends, he asked himself, could he find

one to defend him before the Inquiry? None of them was his true bosom pal.

Eventually he was officially informed of the terms of the charges he would have to face. But the statutory words from Section 7 of the Police Act of 1861 told him nothing. They amounted in effect to the single accusation that he had helped Tiger. And he had done that. And he was going to lie and lie about it. That was enough.

The heat seemed to get worse by a measurable amount each succeeding day. Tempers everywhere were frayed. There were outbreaks of rioting, giving him the empty consolation that at least this year it was not his task to sort out the cause of some particular incident at the behest of an interested politician. Once, on one of the long, aimless walks he took so as to eat away the slow hours, he saw an enraged Muslim pull a sword out of the gupti that had seemed to be his innocent walking-stick and set off in chase after a member of a rival sect. He began to pursue the fellow, but when he saw the quarry was going to escape in any case he gave up. What business was it of his?

In the tingling heat the very crows in the streets were going about with open, gaping beaks. At home crawling columns of black ants came in successive invasions, and each day the kitchen seemed to spawn a new family of avaricious, predatory cockroaches.

There were a few interruptions in this long, blank, time-out-of-life period, with the dull rage ever in the back of his head. Once he had to give evidence in a case at the Esplanade Magistrate's Court, a comparatively trifling affair that for one reason or another had been long delayed. It was to have an unexpected outcome for him, in more ways than one.

He had been involved originally only because the victim of the theft was a person of influence and in consequence Crime Branch had been called in. However, he had not been displeased with the part he had played. It had so happened that no one in that influential victim's home had thought to record just where the Goan servant who had run off with some of the family jewellery had originally lived. But by patiently tracking the fellow back from employer to employer he had at last discovered the exact address and one quick telephone call to his native place had secured his arrest.

Now at the hearing, which should have gone without a hitch, trouble suddenly blew up. The absconding man had been offered the services of a lawyer, a lady barrister belonging to the People's Union for Civil Liberties, an organisation he himself viewed with no little mistrust. And the lady a Mrs Vimala Ahmed, a person of some notoriety in legal and police circles, he again had faint, irrational reservations about as being a Hindu married to a Muslim. Shortly after the accused, who seemed much cowed by the formality of the court, had begun his evidence Mrs Ahmed jumped up and asked him to take off his shirt. And there, plain to see, were the marks of a severe beating.

Ghote, sitting listening after giving his own evidence, cursed the damn fool of a sub-inspector at the local police station who had had custody of the man. There had been no need to get a confession out of him. The case was perfectly strong. And now this . . .

Mrs Ahmed, an unusual figure among Bombay's colourfully dressed women in that she chose always to clothe her not unimpressive, stout person in absolutely plain saris of drab, workmanlike green cotton, relieved now only by the starched white barrister's bands round her bare neck, at once asked to call the sub-inspector to the witness-box. Then with question after question in a tone of finely controlled anger she ripped into him. Each answer showed him more clearly as the stupid brute that he was, and at the climax he even asked, in a voice filled with truculence, 'Was I to feed the fellow chocolate pudding?'

Mrs Ahmed, matronly and magnificent in her outrage, stood back then and simply looked across at the Magistrate.

And he threw the case out there and then.

Ghote had been fuming increasingly as he realised that all his own good work was in more and more danger of going for nothing. He had looked forward to blasting the sub-inspector as soon as the hearing was over with all the fury he had pent up. But when the Magistrate announced his decision a quite different thought shot into his head.

Mrs Ahmed, with all that angry power, would she not make a fine defender in his own case?

She was already leaving the courtroom, having stuffed her papers into a large, battered-looking, shapeless bag of thick leather, which she swung by a broad strap over her shoulder. Without more time for reflection, he moved swiftly to intercept her.

He caught up with her on the steps outside.

'Madam, madam,' he called. 'One word, please, if you would be so good.'

'It is Inspector – You gave evidence. Inspector Ghote. I did not think it worthwhile to cross-examine.'

'No. No, madam, I am glad.'

'Glad you did not have to face what I gave to that evil fellow? Lucky for you, I do not know anything to your detriment.'

Ghote drew himself up.

'There is nothing I have done to be ashamed,' he said.

For a moment he thought Mrs Ahmed was going to challenge the statement. A civil-libertieswalli to the core, she probably believed that each and every police officer was like that brutal fool just now.

But instead a sudden shrewd look appeared on her well-flashed, time-lined face.

'Perhaps you have not done anything to be ashamed of, Inspector,' she said. 'It is easy to think the police are corrupt and brutal from top to bottom when you have seen as much as I have. But exception must be there.'

'Let me kindly assure you such is the case with me.'

'Well, I am happy to believe it. But what can I do for you?'

'You can defend me, madam,' Ghote said. 'I am under suspension.'

As soon as he had spoken the words he wished he had not. Mrs Ahmed's readiness to admit her prejudices had made him see she was a person not only with fire in her belly but with a particular regard for the truth. And, if he was to tell her that, yes, he had done just what he was to be accused of at the coming Inquiry, would she then agree to take up his cause? With the majority of advocates, he knew well, the questions would not arise. They saw the law as if it was a game of chess with only right moves or wrong, with no concern over right and wrong themselves. But Mrs Ahmed, he guessed now, was not a chess player but a worker at life.

'To defend you, Inspector?' she asked in return. 'Well, what is it you are accused of? Let me warn you, I will not take up a case of police brutality or corruption. In the unlikely event of any officer coming to trial on such charges.'

'No,' Ghote answered, feeling every word pushing against the grain. 'It is not any such offence I am charged with. It is a disciplinary matter. A certain senior officer a year ago unlawfully killed a subordinate, and I am charged with aiding the said officer to conceal evidence.'

Mrs Ahmed, erect in her workmanlike drab sari on the steps of the court building in the electrically oppressive heat of the cloud-shrouded day, looked at him fair and squarely.

'And did you aid this officer?' she asked.

'No,' said Inspector Ghote.

The lie hurt him, as if it was a splinter of wood pushed up under one of his nails. But he said to himself that he had to have told it. He doubted if he would find an advocate more likely to fight for him when the Inquiry produced traps and pits to fall into. And to win through unscathed to its end was what he must do if he was to stay as a police officer, to work in the long future as Tiger would have done.

'Then it is a matter of the powers-that-be wishing,' Mrs

Ahmed asked, 'to lift up some blame by also involving a person of junior rank?'

There was very little of the question in her query. And, with only one last instant of inner hesitation, Ghote agreed that her supposition was most probably correct.

'Then you can count on me,' Mrs Ahmed said. 'Up to my level best.'

Making his way slowly home, while overhead the clouds rumbled with outbreaks of thunder that sounded a little less empty than in the past few days, Ghote felt he had taken a step which might at the end of everything lead him out of his maze of trouble.

Then, just as he dismounted from his scooter, there came a tremendous gust of wind, almost knocking over both man and machine and bending the nearby palm trees as if they were no more than reeds. There followed a half minute of awed, mysterious, empty silence with the sky a tense coppery cloud-dome from horizon to horizon. And then came a great double crack of thunder like a warning from the gods and the first monsoon downpour bucketed on to him.

10

With the arrival of the monsoon the remaining weeks until the Inquiry began were yet more stultifyingly aimless for Ghote, despite the ending of the tension-tingling pre-monsoon heat with the advent of the cooling rains. But he was no longer able to get out of the house by taking long walks about the city, like poor retired Inspector D'Sa. The roads he had slowly moved along in the days of stifling heat were often deep under floodwater now, and where they were not blocked by a foot or more of muddy brown water – sometimes no doubt the work of urchins like those he had failed to rebuke – pavements and roadways were frequently swirling with the fast-flowing excess of the walls and walls of warm rain.

Indoors, everything smelt day and night of damp cotton and every surface that could hold mould was, unless Protima had wiped it hard, covered in greeny, pungent fungus. He himself attended each day to his uniform shoes – out of economy they had never had silica pouches – and to the seldom-worn Sam Browne belt that went with his review uniform. It was young Ved's duty, in which with pouncing pleasure he delighted, to wring out at regular intervals the towels placed at the foot of each window to catch the fast-dripping moisture.

Oh yes, Ghote had thought when the boy had done this in former years, he can stick at it also. He would do well.

Out of doors, cars by the hundred were either brought to a halt in the floods or made immobile by damp in their engines. The trains were, as always, frequently unable to run where water covered the rails, and the city's hundreds of thousands of commuters had to struggle in to their offices on foot, trousers rolled to the calf, saris hoisted almost as high, the ends of draped dhotis tucked into jacket pockets, a moving mass of black umbrellas. Gallantly they would manage to reach their destinations often as late as two in the afternoon, by which time it was only sensible to turn round and start off home again.

Houses in the more crowded parts collapsed, pumped into sogginess by the hosing storms. And from the more affluent areas there were stories of flat roofs turned by the torrents into swimming baths that suddenly descended into the rooms below.

But then at last came the letter informing Ghote of the date the Inquiry was to begin. He took out his shoes and belt once more and gave them an extra polish. He got Protima to iron with double care his uniform. And he made an appointment to see Mrs Vimala Ahmed.

She insisted on him coming to the People's Union for Civil Liberties, and the fears he had had about her almost from the moment of making his abrupt request to her to represent him grew sharply more insistent. What did he want with P.U.C.L. trouble-makers? He was a police officer.

However, at the office Mrs Ahmed, dipping every now and again into her sturdy leather bag for a notebook or even a law volume, kept their discussion strictly to practical points. Little by little Ghote found himself coming to admire her. P.U.C.L.-walli she might be, but she was no fluttering butterfly sipping at the showiest flower only. She could work. He felt a link of warmth with her.

'And this man –' She flicked a glance at her notebook. 'This Shivram Patel, you did not see him when you were reaching that house that night about midnight?'

'No,' he answered firmly. 'No, not at all. He was sleeping at the other end of the house altogether. I saw his servant only.'

'Good. Yes. And the servant would give evidence about the exact time of your arrival?'

'Yes. Yes, he must,' Ghote answered, thinking of the trick he had played on the fellow at Tiger's insistence, and wondering whether Mrs Ahmed would turn him out if she knew.

By the day on which the Inquiry started he felt, despite inner qualms, that, with Mrs Ahmed on his side, he must stand a good chance of coming out of it cleared.

The affair was to be held in the Old Secretariat building, looking out stone-faced and British on to the now verdant, puddly expanse of the Oval Maidan. Ghote got there some minutes early, uniform stiff with starch, Sam Browne gleaming with polish, black necktie arranged to a nicety, to meet Mrs Ahmed once more for a last few words of consultation.

She arrived almost as soon as he had, her leather bag bulging more than ever.

'Well, do you know who it is they have chosen as Presiding Officer?' she said at once, bristling with indignation.

'No, no. I have not at all heard.'

'It is S. M. Motabhoy, Deputy Commissioner. Right at the end of his service. Toeing the safe-line policy, busy making up to the politicians hoping for some sinecure retirement job. He will do his level best to get a conviction.'

But Ghote, strung up to a pitch of nervousness in any case, found he was unable to feel any gloomier. Perhaps, he told himself, this is only P.U.C.L. prejudices speaking.

He nodded once, and side by side they marched up the

building's dark stone staircase, along a tall corridor lined with the photographs of past Inspectors-General, many of the frames slightly crooked, and entered the Inquiry room.

At a long table facing the tall windows the five uniformed officers of the Board were already sitting. In the middle was S. M. Motabhoy, a tall, plumpish Parsi, round face impassive behind a pair of moon-like spectacles, belying beneath the well-fitting khaki uniform with its rows of bright medal ribbons the still athletic body of a former fast bowler cricketer.

So this was the man on whom his whole fate would depend, Ghote thought. What if Mrs Ahmed was right and because this distant-looking figure was seeking a soft job his own life would be tumbled to ruin like one of the rain-soaked tenements in the crowded quarters?

Setting his mouth in a grim line, he marched up to the long table, saluted and gave his name.

S. M. Motabhoy coughed softly.

'Good,' he said. 'So it seems we are now all present. There is one minute still, I believe, before our official starting time, but I see no reason why we should not begin.'

He gave Ghote a long look from behind his moony, pale framed spectacles.

'You may be seated, Inspector,' he said.

Ghote looked round, saw a chair evidently meant for the accused and went and sat himself on its edge. Mrs Ahmed made her way to a table behind him and set down her heavy bag on the floor with a decided thump.

Ghote felt it as an act of defiance, and welcomed it.

S. M. Motabhoy coughed again.

'Let me state at the outset,' he said, 'that I see no reason, despite Inspector Ghote having chosen to be legally represented with the consequence that the questions I myself would have put will be asked by a representative of the civil establishment, I see no reason why we should be constrained by the procedures of the civil courts. This is an Inquiry, no more than that. And no less. Let us conduct it in whatever way seems most likely to elicit the truth.'

Ghote, perched on his wooden chair, felt himself prey to mixed emotions.

Was this really the approach of a man determined on getting a sharply disciplinary verdict? It did not altogether seem so. And if Mrs Ahmed was wrong about him, had he himself been right to entrust his case to her? But then there were those concluding words: *to elicit the truth*. What if the Inquiry did, after all, elicit the truth, the factual truth, of what had happened on that night of June 24 a year ago?

And did he, in his heart of hearts, actually want it to?

From outside there came a deep sustained rumble of thunder and, looking towards the windows, he saw against the dark purple of the rainclouds and the tossing heads of the tall royal palms surrounding the Maidan a long jagged fork of lightning descend from sky to earth.

The disquieting omen was followed at once by something more prosaic but perhaps even more daunting. At S. M. Motabhoy's invitation the lawyer presenting the case against rose to his feet from behind a papers-covered table at the opposite end of the big room.

Until that moment Ghote had not seen who it was who had been chosen to counterbalance his own insistence on having the services of a barrister. But when S. M. Motabhoy had called on 'Mr Sankar' a premonition had run through him, and now he saw that the tall, white-haired figure, dressed in a severely elegant black atchkan, twenty-one silver buttons down its length, was indeed R. K. Sankar.

In his late seventies now, 'R.K.', as he was invariably called, had been in the British days a leading fighter for nationalism. But he had not been by any means a champion of non-violence. Instead, marching at the head of avowedly aggressive demonstrations, he had been thrown into gaol time and again. He had been charged with conspiracy to derail trains, to burn Government property, to rob local treasuries and had gloried in not denying the charges. But then had come Independence and, rejected for any official position because of the unfashionableness of his views during the struggle, he had taken up a hitherto neglected career at the Bar. And had seemed to be an utterly different man. Rage apparently exhausted, he had become known up and down the country for the cold logic with which he won his cases and for his unblinking calm when he met his rare defeats. In police circles his name had become a byword as a cross-examiner it was laceration to come up against.

Ghote's spirits sank.

'Gentlemen,' R. K. began now, in a voice that carried quietly clear from one end of the big room to the other. 'The question before you today is a simple one. What we have to ask is no more than this: on the night of June the 24th and 25th last year was Inspector G. V. Ghote, here before you now, derelict in his duty at Vigatpore Police Station in that he assisted the late Additional Deputy Inspector-General of Police B. N. Kelkar in disposing of the body of one Police Sergeant S. R. Desai, unlawfully killed by the said A.D.I.G. Kelkar?'

Transfixed almost as a rabbit under the following silk-smooth laying out of the case against himself, Ghote sat listening to R.K.'s clearly articulating voice as if it was outlining events that had occurred to someone quite other than himself. Someone patently guilty of what was being alleged.

And when, after more than an hour, R.K. sat down and took a single sip of water from the net covered glass on the table beside his papers, he realised that the sum of all that had been said was close enough to the actual events of that night of June 24 to be almost the exact truth.

Yes, he had done all that had been alleged against him. With Tiger Kelkar he had carried the heavily slumped body of that idiot Desai out of the police station at Vigatpore, down in the sheeting rain past the bicycle stable – there

R.K.'s reconstruction had been out: he had had them going straight to the stable – and, once the body was balanced floppily on the machine, the two of them had gone through the edge of the town and down to the muddy shore of Lake Helena. And, yes, he himself had found a boat there, had helped Tiger heave into it the now undressed body with its head wound battered into disguise, and with him had paddled laboriously through the dark to somewhere out near the middle of the lake and there they had lowered the body into the black water. Where face-down it had floated obscenely.

Yes, all that he had actually done. And R.K. in his calm, dispassionate tones had told the Inquiry of it, as if he had been, a hovering spirit from the icy Himalayas, witness of every hurried, snatched-at move.

How had so much been found out about what he alone, now that Tiger was dead, could know? It was almost unbelievable. It was frightening.

He hardly heard S. M. Motabhoy say that he thought there would be no harm in taking a luncheon adjournment rather early at this point. Mrs Ahmed had, in fact, to tap him smartly on the shoulder to rouse him.

'I have some business to see to in the lunch period,' she said. 'There are some slums dwellers out at Worli whose huts were washed away and some of them have been arrested for sleeping in the stairways of a block of exclusive flats opposite. But I will be back well before the adjournment is over.'

'Oh. Oh, yes. Yes. Thank you.'

Mrs Ahmed, slinging her bag on her shoulder, turned to go.

'Wait. Please. Please, wait. I am wanting to – To ask . . .'

'Yes? What is it? Other people are depending on me besides yourself, you know.'

Ghote licked at his lips.

'All I am wanting to know,' he said miserably, 'is should I

after all say I am guilty? There seems to be so much evidence against me.'

Mrs Ahmed's eyes lit with anger.

'Evidence?' she said. 'Nonsense. Up to now, Inspector, as you should know, they have not produced one jot or tittle of evidence. Let R.K. bring his witnesses, and then let me put them to the proof. After that we shall see.'

'Yes,' said Ghote. 'Yes, of course. Thank you.'

He was aware that he had sounded feeble. But, for all the battlesome reassurance Mrs Ahmed had given him, he knew that he had indeed done almost everything the great R. K. had said that he had done. So how could he truly claim he was not guilty? That he was, as he had allowed Mrs Ahmed to believe, only the destined scapegoat for a senior officer's inadmissable wrongdoing.

He rode despondently home for his lunch through the steadily pouring rain, past the slow tides and counter-tides of black umbrellas. Forcing down the special meal Protima had prepared, his favourite monsoon mushrooms and potato, he scarcely spoke a word.

11

Back at the Inquiry, Ghote found that he had arrived a little early. Mrs Ahmed, too, had managed to return from her visit to the rained-out slum dwellers at Worli before the start of the day's second session. Ghote felt he ought to take the opportunity of asking her how matters had gone. He owed it to her to be interested after the way she had rebuked him for demanding her full attention for himself earlier. And, besides, it would do no harm to gain more of the sympathies of his formidable defender.

He turned from his chair.

'Madam,' he said, 'I trust your visit to Worli was one hundred percent successful.'

'No, Inspector, it was not.'

No trace of the answering pleasure he had hoped for on her solid countenance.

'Oh. Oh, well, I am most sorry to hear.'

He turned away. Further details of what had aroused Mrs Ahmed's wrath were perhaps best avoided.

'No, Inspector,' her voice came from behind him, 'I regret to tell you that your colleagues at the police station there were altogether as unyielding as I had expected.'

Reluctantly Ghote turned back to her.

'Well, nevertheless,' he said, 'perhaps they were having some quantity of right on their side. Not each and every slumdweller is a first-class saint, you know.'

'Oh, I am not needing you to tell me that, Inspector. I have met more slumdwellers myself, I believe, than you have seen even.'

Ghote felt a little offended.

'Madam, a police officer is often and often having to deal with the lowest types of humanity.'

'Stop, stop, Inspector. A typical policewalla's attitude is there. Just because a man or woman is poor of the poorest you are always thinking they are bound to be criminal also.'

'Madam, not at all, not at all.'

'Yes, Inspector.'

Ghote felt an uprush of indignation at this implacable answer. Of indignation divided equally between himself and her. Indignation with her because her attitude was, he felt, typical too, typical of a P.U.C.L.-walli. Indignation with himself because his plan to please his defender seemed to have brought about, disastrously, the exactly opposite result.

'Madam, I am saying, we in the police are not at all having such attitudes.'

He knew the all-embracing claim was false even as he made it, but he could produce no other response.

'Very well, Inspector, if that is what you are believing, then I suggest you come out with me to Worli this evening when once more I have to go to see these poor people. At that place you will learn for yourself.'

There was nothing he wanted to do less. By the end of the day, he knew, having listened to the first of the long parade of witnesses R. K. Sankar would call against him, he would want only to get back as soon as he could through the rain and the tides of black umbrella-weaving crowds to the safety and sanity of his own home. But Mrs Ahmed's challenge had been issued, and for the honour of the good there was in the police service he could do no other than take it up.

'Very well, madam,' he said, 'I shall be very much pleased to accompany when proceedings here are over.'

The first witness R. K. Sankar called provided no evidence for Mrs Ahmed to object to. He was no more significant a person than Tiger Kelkar's former orderly, who had had the unfortunate experience of finding Tiger's body, hand still grasping the heavy Service revolver. Thus he had been the first to see the note Tiger had left. Once this had been identified and sworn to, his part in the Inquiry was ended. Mrs Ahmed let him go unquestioned.

S. M. Motabhoy undertook to read the note aloud himself.

With a lurch of dismay, Ghote saw, as it was taken across to the Board table, Tiger's familiar handwriting on the sheets of buff official notepaper, as vigorous and spiky as the man himself.

Tiger, he thought, I wanted you to be able to go on being that strong cleansing self. And I wanted to try to become such a fiery force for good myself. And I still will become that force.

If I get out of this.

He listened unswervingly as the words of Tiger's confession, unheard by him till now, fell into the silent attentive room, with only the steady swishing of the rain outside as background. And though the words were delivered not in Tiger's sharp bark but in S. M. Motabhoy's rounded, fruity tones, he felt as he heard them that Tiger, indeed, was there present.

An encouraging ghost.

And certainly Tiger had done his best to omit his helper's part in the events of that disastrous night.

'. . . found that the man Desai had expired . . . I realise now . . . decided to dispose of the body as best I could . . . conveying it with considerable difficulty on my own . . . placed the garments in the Muddamal Room at the station,

104

intending at a later time . . . would like to express my deep regret . . .'

As soon as the reading was over R.K. rose to his feet.

'It will be my case, of course,' he said, 'that the account which you have just heard is incorrect in one substantial particular. A.D.I.G. Kelkar did not, as he stated, carry out this illegal action unaided.'

Yes, Ghote thought, that is so.

But, with Tiger's fire-breathing presence still hovering, he felt more determined than he had yet been that he would fight it out. As he could. As he could. Only he himself and dead Tiger knew for certain what had taken place that night. All the guesswork R.K. had embarked on, or had had constructed for him, was no more than a series of clever suppositions.

No one besides himself knew the truth, and he had only to do one thing: cling hard to his determination not to let that truth out.

R.K.'s next witnesses did not test his resolution to any great extent. They were the personnel from Vigatpore Police Station whom, on that distant night, he had one by one sent off duty. He saw why R.K. was bringing them in, one after the other. Their successive evidence showed simply but with a completeness which from a professional standpoint he could only applaud that by 11 p.m. that night the station had been deserted except for the sentry outside, the peon Shinde, Tiger Kelkar, himself and Sergeant Desai.

Mrs Ahmed shot to her feet more than once while the procession of witnesses went by. But Ghote soon realised that her interventions were no more than tiny skirmishes in the war she and he were fighting. Yet he did not feel disheartened. Skirmishes they might be, but each was a sign that the war was being fought. There would be no surrender.

The afternoon wore on. Outside, the slapping rain slackened to a drizzle, then came down with renewed intensity, then slackened again. Once or twice, lulled by its sound when it was at its least noisy, Ghote actually found himself dropping into a near-doze.

And once, when through the tall windows he saw in the distance out over the sea somewhere a delicate tracery of lightning flicker down, his mind wandered so far from the proceedings as to recall and linger over a piece of poetry he had learnt as a boy. He had learnt it not at school but from that best friend of his, the son of the village pandit, the boy with the tremendous temper, Ram. Ram had heard it somewhere and because it was 'dirty' had eagerly passed it on. It was from an ancient poet of the uninhibited days, from the sixth century or so, if he remembered rightly, Subandhu. 'Lightning like a row of nail marks left upon the cloud by its lover, the departing day.'

With a jerk he was roused from that reverie by the sound of a name deeply familiar to him, a name from his past, though a more recent past than those boyhood days of his swapping pieces of possibly dirty poetry with Ram Bhaskar.

'. . . would like next to call Inspector G. P. Nadkarni, former Inspector Nadkarni, I should say.'

The icily articulating voice of R.K.

And the witness he was intending to call: Inspector Nadkarni, now long retired, once his mentor when he had first joined the C.I.D., the man from whom he had learnt so much that was truly useful. The little things that no lectures at Detective School could teach nor any textbooks, not even that of the great Dr Hans Gross, adapted by John Adam, Crown and Public Prosecutor, Madras, still reposing as ever in his Headquarters cabin.

Old Nadkarni, his mentor.

Why was R.K. calling him? But, no sooner had he asked himself the question, than the answer came to him. Nadkarni was being called because at the period years before when he himself had had most to do with Tiger, when he had first developed the admiration he felt for him, Nadkarni had been working with them both. So he could testify, better than anyone, to that admiration, that hero-worship.

And if R.K. could show convincingly how deeply he had admired Tiger then, he would have established that he had a very good motive for having aided and assisted him in Vigatpore.

He felt a new quiver of apprehension.

Whoever had prepared the case against him for R.K. had done his work with fearful thoroughness. What else unexpected would he have found evidence of?

But S. M. Motabhoy, impassive in the middle of the Board table, gave now a resounding, fruity cough of interruption.

'Mr Sankar,' he said, 'I have been looking at my watch. It is high time. I think we had better adjourn before you call this next witness.'

'As you please,' R.K. murmured.

So, with no further formality, all of them in the big, high-ceilinged room packed up their papers, rose to their feet, here and there stretched discreetly and left – the first day's proceedings ended.

Mrs Ahmed, however, came marching up to Ghote.

'Well, Inspector, are you going to come with me to Worli? Or have you had some mind-change?'

He had nurtured a tiny hope that their spat of an altercation at the start of the session would have been forgotten, together with his promise. But he was not going to be seen as backing down.

'Yes, I am ready to go,' he said. 'But first only I must telephone my wife to say I would be late.'

'Very well. I mean to catch the Number 44 bus. You can meet me at the bus stand.'

This was another blow. He had imagined that they would go up to Worli by taxi, with Mrs Ahmed paying. But evidently she was determined not to expend more than the barest minimum on her mission. Or, he thought with a squirt of savagery as he came away from giving his explanation to

Protima, perhaps it was just that she was determined to make her P.U.C.L. path seem as stony as possible.

He stepped out into the steadily teeming rain, letting the rancorous misery he had begun to feel rapidly take over the whole of his mind.

Even the luck they had at the bus stand – the second No 44 to arrive had room on board – did nothing to dispel his gloom. Throughout the long buffeting journey, up past the docks, through the mills area, the tall blank walls to either side drearily washed by the sweeping palls of rain, and across at last to Worli itself, he sat in fixed silence. On the windows of the jam-packed bus the steam of humanity condensed in water drops that ran endlessly down to wet the seat beside him.

Mrs Ahmed, too, appeared lost in thought. Though, whenever he ventured a quick look towards her, he surmised that it was not dejected misery like himself she was feeling but rather a steadily mounting anger at the prospect of the difficulties she was going to experience.

At last they arrived.

'First to the police station,' Mrs Ahmed said, decisively as if she was a senior officer – almost Tiger Kelkar himself – issuing orders. 'Then we must go to the wives of these men in the slum where they have been found somewhere to stay in other huts.'

'Very good,' said Ghote dully.

Drearily he tramped along beside the stout figure of the P.U.C.L. stalwart, her raised umbrella though it was large only partially sheltering him.

The police station, when they squelched up to it, seemed to answer all his worst forebodings. The Station House Officer, a big, glowingly corpulent sub-inspector, declared brazenly that he had no knowledge of the men who had been arrested at the posh flats where they had taken refuge. So far as he was concerned there were no such people.

'But I tell you I was seeing them this morning itself,' Mrs

Ahmed said, drawing herself up for battle. 'Are you saying they have been let go free, Mr Sub-Inspector? Or is it that they have been so much maltreated that you are not daring to let a member of the legal profession see?'

The colour rose on the sub-inspector's well-fleshed cheeks.

'Madam, I am saying you have no damn business here.'

Ghote, who had been hovering back near the doorway, more than a little willing to disassociate himself from these P.U.C.L. matters, took an impulsive step forward.

'S.I.,' he said, 'I am with this lady. Ghote, Crime Branch.'

He was conscious, even as he spoke, that he was wearing uniform only by special dispensation for the Inquiry period and that, a suspended officer, it was straining a point even to claim he came from Headquarters. But the fellow's attitude, vindicating at once Mrs Ahmed's claims about police behaviour, brought up in him a brushfire of bad temper which had cracklingly swept away all discretion.

The sub-inspector looked up from his desk.

'Oh, if it is Crime Branch matter,' he said with evident sullenness, 'then go ahead, Inspector, do what you damn well like.'

Led by Mrs Ahmed, Ghote marched then into the station and through to the lock-up, conscious of holding himself more upright than usual.

The lock-up was neither worse nor better than most. But, seeing it through Mrs Ahmed's eyes, Ghote felt a certain shame. There were some fifty men and boys confined in the narrow space between its grease-blackened walls and the stink of mere humanity, of urine and ordure, rolled heavily out in the humid air. Seeing his uniform, four or five of the prisoners who had been clutching the narrow bars which formed the whole outer wall retreated swiftly towards the interior darkness, plainly expecting blows if not worse.

Others, more sanguine, less used to police-station life, pressed forward at the sight of Mrs Ahmed's sari, extending naked arms through the bars, squeezing naked chests as near to freedom and the outside world as they could get.

Happily, Mrs Ahmed recognised among them her own particular clients and, it seemed, she was bringing them comparatively good news. She had arranged, she said, for them to be represented when they were brought before the magistrate and she had also found temporary accommodation for their families .

'We are going to see now,' she reassured them. 'And since one of our lawyers will be present when you are brought to court you can be sure that at most you will be fined. Then you can rejoin your wives.'

But her words did not seem to bring as much comfort as they might have been expected to do, and Mrs Ahmed turned away, stopping to scrape some filth off one of her chappals, unthanked.

Out in the rain again, making their way towards the slum where the huts that had disintegrated had been, Ghote felt bold enough to comment on the limited success of the visit.

'Madam, I was sorry to observe that what you were doing for these people was not earning you very much of kudos.'

'No, Inspector. These people are too much downtrodden to have many feelings, whether gratitude for what little anyone does for them or anger at the many things that are done against them. And you should be happy at that. If they were as altogether enraged as they ought to be, you policewallas would have nothing else to do from morning to night but attempt to put down rioting.'

'Well, yes, I am seeing that. But, madam, all the same I was wondering . . .'

'What wondering, Inspector?'

'Oh, madam, why at all are you doing such work? Madam, if I may say it, here you are, an educated lady who could be having a fine job, if domestic duties are not making too much of calls upon your time. But instead you are doing this. Madam, why is that?'

Mrs Ahmed turned her head under her big dripping umbrella and looked at him.

'I am surprised that you ask, Inspector.'

'Why surprised, madam?'

Mrs Ahmed gave him a somewhat wry smile.

'Because I do not think of policemen showing very much of concern about others, Inspector, if it is the truth you are wanting.'

Ghote felt too abashed to reply. He skipped over a large yellowy brown puddle and walked on, his question unanswered.

'Well,' Mrs Ahmed said after they had gone in silence for some hundred yards, 'I will tell you, Mr Ghote, how it all came about.'

For a moment more she was silent, gathering her thoughts.

'I am country-born, you know,' she began at last. 'My father was a landowner, we are a well-to-do family. But not at all educated. My mother was never English-speaking, and my father spoke it always quite badly. So when –'

She came to a halt. But, Ghote thought, this was not solely because they had come to a crossing and the rain-swirling gutter needed some care to negotiate.

On the far side she stopped and turned to face him. He stepped a little closer to gain what shelter he could from her sturdy umbrella.

'Mr Ghote,' she said, plunging in, 'I had a brother, one year younger, and you, you may imagine, how pleased and proud I was to be his didi, to teach and protect him. And then – Then one day he was seen to have leprosy. Yes, in our good, clean, rich family we had a leper. This was long ago, mind you, in the pre-Independence days. And so . . . So my parents at once believed that their small son had committed in his past life some sin so altogether vile that it would be sin in them also to so much as touch him or talk to him. And they sent this little bright boy – he was ten years of age only – to a

111

distant, distant leper colony. It was as if he had died suddenly. Worse, even.'

She swirled abruptly round.

'But we must not linger,' she said. 'I will tell you the rest while we walk.'

'If you do not want,' Ghote said, 'kindly remain silent.'

'No, I would like you to hear. I feel sometimes that you are not altogether well disposed to P.U.C.L. people, Inspector, and I would like you to know how one of them came to join.'

'But – But I assure –'

'No. No need, Inspector. Listen only.'

'Very well, madam.'

'At first when my jewel brother was taken away like that I was bitterly angry. Angry with the gods, angry with my father and mother. Angry with everyone and everything. But after one year I thought that I had to go and see this brother who had been lifted out of our lives. So I asked and requested and altogether badgered my parents, and at last they consented to go on pilgrimage to Rishikesh where they had sent my Vasudev. You know where is Rishikesh, Inspector?'

'Yes, yes. It is in the foothills of the Himalayas.'

'Well, there when we went I at last found my little brother. He was a beggar, Inspector. Clothed in rags, squatting by the bridge that is there, crying and whining for the alms which people wishing to acquire merit threw from a safe distance. Well, Inspector, twelve years of age only though I was, it did not take me one minute then to make up my mind that something had to be done. And I asked and asked and made myself a thorough nuisance to one and all, and at last I found that there was nearby a good, clean colony where lepers were not seen as outcasts but were helped to live a decent life. And I made my parents take Vasudev to that place.'

She had been walking at a tremendous rate, splashing regardlessly through puddles and slime. Ghote, beside her, had been aware that his trousers were getting extremely muddy, if not to the fearful extent they had got to be on his terrible march with Tiger Kelkar.

But now she slowed and looked at him again.

'Well, from that day on, Inspector,' she said, 'I knew what I had to do in this world. To fight for the poor and to fight against all hypocrisies.'

'Yes, madam,' Ghote said.

And he tramped onwards in thoughtful silence.

They arrived at the slum, a collection of lopsided patchy constructions of the inevitable beaten-out tins and jaggedy pieces of polythene sheeting, perched crazily on the steep side of a small hill overlooking the sea. On the opposite side of the wide road were the big pink, green and yellow blocks of the posh flats in the stairways of which the families whose huts had been washed away had taken illicit refuge.

A few sodden goats and two cows slowly disputed over some edible strands of something on a huge rubbish heap at the foot of the slope.

They entered the area. From hut to hut Mrs Ahmed went, slipping and sliding on the narrow earth paths, deep now in glutinous mud. Time and again she dipped her head low, pushing aside a dripping rag that served as a hut door, and inquired of the wretched people huddled inside – more than once Ghote saw a whole family crouched on a charpoy out of a sullen flood on the floor, holding pieces of cardboard over their heads against leaks – where the families of the men in the lock-up were to be found.

They located them at last and, to Ghote's shamed relief, Mrs Ahmed told him then that she felt he had seen enough.

'Well, goodbye, madam,' he said. 'Until the Inquiry tomorrow.'

Soaked and sombre, he made his way, by two different buses, back home. He said nothing to Protima of the reason for his lateness, and that night he dreamt that he had become a leper.

12

Setting off for the Inquiry next morning, pressed uniform protected from the dolloping rain by a voluminous cape, Duck Back gumboots replacing polished shoes for the journey, Ghote found it hard to believe it was all such a life-and-death business as up to now he had believed it to be.

But it was not long before once again he found he was fully caught up.

As soon as S. M. Motabhoy and his fellow Board members had taken their places R. K. Sankar's next promised witness, former Inspector Nadkarni, was ushered in by the Inquiry orderly.

He walked across to the witness table with some show of the smart police officer of old. But Ghote saw with sudden sadness that since they had last seen each other Nadkarni had lost almost everything of the inward vitality he had once possessed, very different from Tiger Kelkar's aggressiveness but unmistakably there. White-haired now and markedly round-shouldered, his face behind the familiar pair of gold-rimmed spectacles of the last years of his service was plainly withered, the cheeks paunchy and slack.

But, whatever changes there were in his appearance, he must be still the Nadkarni of old, his mentor, kind always yet unsparing in quiet criticism when such had been his due. There would come, if at any time he had said or done something even a little foolish, a small dry cough, a steady, mild but inescapable look and some such words as 'Not altogether wise, I think.' A rebuke more effective than any shouted abuse.

R. K. Sankar rose now from his papers-covered table smoothly as a cobra, his long black atchkan elegantly uncreased as ever, its row of silver buttons softly glinting.

'You are Mr G. P. Nadkarni, formerly an inspector of police, Bombay Crime Branch?'

'I am.'

The voice, Ghote heard with dismay, had now the faintest quaver in it.

'You have, since your retirement for the police service, occupied the onerous position of Head of Security at the Bombay office of the Reserve Bank of India?'

'I did occupy that post, but I have finally retired since the past one year.'

'I see. But you would agree that among the many qualities required in such a responsible position is the ability to make sound judgements concerning a variety of different people?'

Nadkarni gave the little cough which Ghote remembered so well. 'Yes, that would be an asset, though I would not claim that I myself possessed it in particular abundance.'

'You are too modest, Mr Nadkarni. But let us move on to the particular matter in which you have agreed to assist us. You were in the past, I understand, a close colleague of Inspector Ghote, now before this Inquiry?'

Nadkarni did not answer immediately.

Ghote, sitting tensely on his hard wooden chair, asked himself if this could be because he knew that what he would have to say would be harmful to himself. Because he was sure that old Nadkarni had liked him, had done his best for him in the past, had been almost a father to him.

Oh, if only he had still been in the service. Then there would have been a brother officer to whom he could have entrusted his defence without a second thought. Only Nadkarni, surely, would never have agreed to defend him were he to have been told the guilty facts.

'I did work with Inspector Ghote, yes.'

'At one time in particular you were, I understand, close colleagues?'

'Yes. That could be said. We were both members of a cell recruited to launch a drive against black-money transactions.'

'And the late A.D.I.G. Kelkar was also a member of this cell or squad?'

'He was.'

'So you would have had many opportunities of observing Inspector Ghote's relations with Inspector Kelkar, as he was at that time?'

'We were all much in each other's company, yes.'

'Would you care to describe for the benefit of this Inquiry what in your view were the relations between Inspectors Ghote and Kelkar?'

Again Nadkarni was silent.

But, Ghote thought, this is the moment when he will have to bring the first log to my funeral pyre. And he hesitates to do it.

'I think Ghote had a great respect for Kelkar, as a more experienced officer.'

'An experienced man who was setting him an example of all that a first-class police officer should be?'

'Yes. You could be saying that.'

'You would say that Inspector Ghote had the greatest admiration for this man, soon to be promoted to a higher rank and with a fine record already behind him?'

'Yes. Yes, that was so.'

Nadkarni, letting his round shoulders sag yet more, looked down at the bare table in front of him.

'Perhaps you would go so far as to characterize Ghote's attitude as a guru-chela relationship?'

Once more Nadkarni hesitated, weighing what words he could utter.

'No. No, I would not go quite as far as that. Ghote certainly admired Kelkar. We all did. He was even then a much respected officer. But I do not think that Ghote regarded himself quite as a disciple, nor Kelkar exactly as a teacher.'

R.K. thoughtfully lowered himself on to his chair, evidently thinking he had got as much out of his witness as he was likely to get, and that it was enough.

Ghote turned and whispered urgently to Mrs Ahmed behind him.

She rose to her feet.

'Mr Nadkarni, one question only. Would you in fact say that if Inspector Ghote had any sort of a guru-chela relationship it existed between yourself and him?'

Nadkarni looked up and gave her a smile of great sweetness.

'Yes,' he said. 'Yes, I was perhaps something of a guru to Ghote when he first joined duty in the C.I.D. And I may say that he made an excellent chela, quick to learn and eager to carry out each and every allotted task.'

'Thank you, Mr Nadkarni.'

The words of praise, in that voice which so sadly had in it all too obviously the quaver of old age, went like an arrow into Ghote's heart. He had hoped in the past that this, or something like it, was what Nadkarni might feel about him. But in those days his mentor had never spoken openly in such a way. And to hear himself praised now, when he was in the very act of behaving in a way Nadkarni certainly would not have given his blessing to: it was a moment of biting shame.

But R.K. had stood to put another question, doubtless feeling that Mrs Ahmed had significantly eroded the impression he hoped he had created.

'Mr Nadkarni, I am sorry to detain you further, but I would like to give you the opportunity to make your opinion perfectly clear. Am I right in understanding, although perhaps the term guru-chela relationship is not quite accurate in describing the high regard which Inspector Ghote had for Mr Kelkar, that at the time we are referring to Ghote did indeed feel for this officer, senior to him in age, experience and success, something not far short of reverence?'

I did, Ghote thought. Yes, that was what I felt for him then. Reverence. And I felt it yet more when he came to Vigatpore.

This time Nadkarni did not hesitate to answer. But his answer was clearly not what R.K. had expected. Nor was it what Ghote had dreaded. The old man's sagging cheeks darkened.

'Really,' he said, his voice rising in a pettish squeak, 'I have given you my answers. Both to you, sir, and to the lady representing Inspector Ghote. I cannot be asked to repeat and repeat what I have already stated.'

It was an outburst, like a late flurry of monsoon rain, that was so uncharacteristic of the Nadkarni that Ghote had known, and so much respected, that he could hardly believe what he had heard. That the man who never to his knowledge had betrayed a single sign of loss of temper, who had been a perfect example of pure patience as an investigating officer, should have been brought down to this display of weak rage: it was a blow almost as sharp as the knowledge of how much Nadkarni would have disapproved of the course he was here and now taking.

'Very well, Mr Nadkarni,' R.K. said, unmoved. 'I shall not press you.'

Hesitantly old Nadkarni made his way over to the door, walking almost as if he might need a stick. At the Board table there was a buzz of consultation. Then, tall and authoritative, S. M. Motabhoy turned and addressed the room.

'Mr Sankar,' he said, his confident, rich tones contrasting

poignantly with Nadkarni's irate screech of only a few moments before. 'Mr Sankar, we feel that the matter you have brought to our notice is of some importance. We need to know, in so far as we can, just what regard Inspector Ghote felt for A.D.I.G. Kelkar, both a year ago and at the most distant time you have been asking about. Would you now, therefore, kindly direct some questions to Inspector Ghote himself.'

Ghote felt shocked. He had realised that at some stage he would have to face R.K.'s famous lashing tongue. But he had assumed this would come only towards the end of the Inquiry, days away. But to have to stand up to it now. It was as if he had been suddenly knocked off his feet by a whirling wind gust.

It seemed that Mrs Ahmed had, too, made the same assumption about when he was to be called.

'Mr Presiding Officer,' she protested, 'my client and I have not even discussed whether he is to go into the witness-box. This is monstrous.'

'Madam,' S. M. Motabhoy replied, blank faced behind his moon-like spectacles. 'Let me repeat what I saw fit to say at the outset of this Inquiry. We are not met as a court of law. Indeed, there is no witness-box as such for your client to go into. This is an inquiry only, an inquiry for the purpose of ascertaining what exactly occurred in Vigatpore on the night of June the 24th and the early hours of June 25th last year. As such we feel it right that questions should be put to Inspector Ghote at whatever stage of our deliberations seems appropriate.'

He turned to R.K. without waiting to see if Mrs Ahmed had resumed her seat or not.

'Mr Sankar.'

R.K. rose, more than ever putting Ghote in mind of a cobra rearing itself sinuously up, hood expanding, forked tongue ready to strike with cold venom.

Stiffly, Ghote rose to his own feet and presented himself rigidly at attention.

'Well now, Inspector,' R.K. said in quietly conversational tones. 'We have heard that you and the late A.D.I.G. Kelkar were some years ago close colleagues. Is that correct?'

'Yes, sir.'

No possibility of denying that. It was a tiny relief to be able to answer one question with complete truth.

'You were, in fact, both members of what, I understand, was called the Black-money and Allied Transactions Squad?'

'Yes, sir.'

Another plain fact.

'But your own duties in that organisation were a little different from those of the other officers?'

'Yes, sir. Yes, I suppose that they were.'

Ghote had answered with more hesitation. It was indeed a fact that he had been seconded to the squad more to seek out an officer giving away its secrets than to work directly at its main task. But he felt that this was entering unexpectedly on a more dubious area.

'Good, Inspector. And it was, was it not, your particular duty to suspect the then Inspector Kelkar of corruptly betraying confidential information?'

Ghote could not stop himself pausing noticeably now before he answered. But without too much delay he brought out his reply.

'Yes, sir. It was my given duty to suspect Mr Kelkar. But also –'

'Yes, to suspect Mr Kelkar. Falsely to suspect him. So, tell us, Inspector, did you not feel that having regarded an officer of such high repute as being capable of committing a most serious crime, a crime that would strike at the very heart of the police service, did you not feel you were bound afterwards to offer him some compensation?'

'Sir,' Ghote answered, his held-in determination at last breaking out. 'Sir, it was not only Inspector Kelkar, as he was then, that it was my duty to suspect. It was each and every member of the squad.'

R.K. gave a long weary sigh.

'Inspector, we are not asking you about your feelings at that distant time. They are of no concern to us whatsoever. What we are asking is whether, when the later A.D.I.G. Kelkar was unfortunate enough to kill a subordinate in a moment of reckless anger, you then recalled that you had owed him over a period of many years a debt of honour.'

Ghote felt a spurt of justified rage at this blatant attempt to blacken him.

'No, sir,' he answered with stone-block firmness. 'Mr Kelkar when he was first meeting me at Vigatpore had said that our former relationship would have no bearing on present matters, and I was happy also to put the past into the past.'

'No doubt you were, Inspector,' R.K. said blandly. 'But let us return to that period when you and Mr Kelkar were close colleagues. During that time when you had many opportunities of observing how Inspector Kelkar, as he then was, went about his work, you developed towards him a certain attitude?'

Another trap here, plainly. But not one it was easy to see a way of not entering.

'A certain attitude, sir?'

'Yes, Inspector.' A long drawn sigh. 'Surely a man of your intelligence, a C.I.D. officer, must know what I mean.'

'Yes, sir.'

'Then, Inspector, kindly provide an answer.'

Ghote licked his dry upper lip with the merest tip of his tongue.

'I was – Well, sir, naturally I admired Inspector Kelkar.'

'Yes, Inspector, you admired him. You wished that you could emulate him?'

Ghote swallowed. He felt that the five members of the Board sitting intently at their long table must have seen his adam's apple rise and fall in his throat. That was always taken to be the sign that a lie had been told. Or was about to be told.

His answer, when at last he brought it out, came with a rush.

'Yes, sir. I did wish to emulate. Inspector Kelkar was a Number One model investigator.'

'So you admired Inspector Kelkar – I understand he was frequently given the sobriquet "Tiger" – you admired Tiger Kelkar and you wished to emulate him. You did your best to emulate him?'

'Yes, sir,' Ghote answered, not seeing how else he could answer.

'Would it be fair to call such an attitude, from someone rather junior to a senior, a guru-chela relationship, Inspector?'

Caught. Transfixed. Like a fish on a hook, dangling and wriggling in the air for everyone to see.

'I – I do not know. Perhaps that is the way you are liking to put.'

'Ah, but, Inspector, is it the way that you would put it? That is what the Inquiry wishes to know. Did you consider yourself to be an ever-faithful chela to A.D.I.G. Kelkar?'

What to answer? It was true really. He had considered himself Tiger's chela, though never in just those words. But Tiger certainly had been everything that he thought he ought to be himself. It had been because of this that he had been so ready to offer him, when the thought had suddenly blossomed within him, that way of escape from the appalling entanglement that had, out of nowhere, enmeshed him. But to this he could not admit.

He swallowed again. And again cursed the tell-tale gulp of his adam's apple.

'Sir, I did not even say that I was Tig – That I was a chela to Mr Kelkar.'

'No, you did not say it. But you felt it nonetheless, did you not?'

And in that instant Ghote thought *I do not care: I will tell the truth. Touch gold and say truth.*

'Yes, sir. I did feel in the end that Tiger Kelkar was my guru, and I was proud if I could be his chela.'

Behind him he heard Mrs Ahmed give a little, half-suppressed gasp. But he could not tell whether it was of dismay or of approval.

R.K. Sankar sat down then with all the dramatic sudden-ness he was accustomed to use in the criminal courts. And, as soon as he was sure his action had made its effect, he rose to his feet again.

'I would like next,' he said, 'to call one Sitaram Shinde, peon at Vigatpore Police Station. But I understand, Mr Presiding Officer, that he will not arrive in Bombay until this evening.'

'But you have other witnesses?' S. M. Motabhoy asked.

'Yes, Mr Presiding Officer. But we have made a good deal more progress than I anticipated and they are not yet ready.'

'Very well then, we shall have to adjourn until tomorrow.'

Ghote, back on his hard little chair again, felt a new dart of anxiety. Shinde, loyal, simple, splay-fingered saluting Shinde, would it still be within his powers to cooperate in the deceit he had asked him to agree to all that time ago? Certainly he must have repeated the lie when Inspector Sawant had been in Vigatpore. But, summoned all the way to Bombay, finding himself in the awe-inspiring surround-ings of the Old Secretariat, symbol of British might and power of old, would he continue to persevere?

Tomorrow was going to be a bad day.

13

Next morning, when on the radio Ghote had heard, not surprisingly, that twelve inches of rain had fallen in the previous twenty-four hours, he arrived at the Inquiry hot and bothered. His scooter had come to a halt in a new foot-deep puddle and he had thought he was going to be late and might even find his former peon – he did not know – already being questioned by R. K. Sankar. Perhaps even the fellow would have broken down under that formidable examination.

But in fact it was just on the stroke of ten when he entered the big room and, to his surprise and sweat-pouring relief, there was no sign of the proceedings even being about to begin. Poor Shinde was nowhere to be seen. R.K. and the four junior officers of the Board were chatting together in low voices. Mrs Ahmed was standing at her table rummaging in her big bag, the shorthand writer was sitting glumly at his desk.

Ghote went up to Mrs Ahmed.

'I am sorry if I am late,' he said. 'There was a waterlogging and my scooter engine died.'

'Nothing to worry,' Mrs Ahmed answered. 'S. M. Motabhoy has been delayed also. He was telephoning to say he would be late by some time. I do not know for what reason.'

'Well, that is a fine piece of luck for me.'

He leant forward nearer her and spoke more quietly.

'I am sorry for what I was saying under R.K.'s questioning yesterday, about Tiger Kelkar and what I was feeling about him. It was the entire truth, and I was not able to hide.'

Mrs Ahmed glanced up from the papers-thick mess in her bag.

'No. It was much best for you to speak up. In the end the truth is always best.'

The truth is always best, he thought dismally. Mrs Ahmed so plainly had made that an article of faith, and he was cheating her. Worse, he was letting her put his lie before the Inquiry with all the force which believing it to be a truth gave to her.

He turned away and went and sat, hunched, on his chair, though he knew that by the end of a long day its hard surface would be a misery to him.

Almost at once he started feeling furious that the session had been delayed. It was all very well for senior officers to decide at their own sweet will that they would come late. Probably S. M. Motabhoy was visiting some shops, perhaps to a tailor to be measured up for a suit to wear when he landed his soft job after retirement. Or he might be spending some time at a health club having massage. He had had all the afternoon yesterday unexpectedly free also.

And all the while here he was sitting waiting for poor Shinde to appear, wondering how he would come up to fierce examination. There was no reason, after all, why he should back up to the hilt the story about not seeing him when he had come back from Lake Helena that night. He himself had done nothing to entitle him to the fellow's good opinion. Except once, giving him the single cigarette Desai had sent him to buy and had not been there to smoke.

Would the fellow commit perjury for one cigarette only?

But he had been devoted as he was long before that night. For whatever reason, he had taken this liking to him. And it had seemed to be cent per cent.

Time passed. Ghote shifted about on his chair. R.K. and the officers of the Board appeared content to chat away. Mrs Ahmed, ignoring them, had settled down to study a clutch of documents she had taken from her bag.

In amongst them Ghote saw that morning's *Indian Express* and after a little, since there was still no sign of S. M. Motabhoy, he asked if he could borrow it. Desultorily he read over the headlines, *Three Die in Police Firing, Pharmacists on Indefinite Strike, PM Urges National Unity.* But they did not catch his interest. What did the ups and downs of national life signify when there hung over his whole career this black cloud, blacker even than the thick pall above them now sending the heavy warm rain tumbling and tumbling down?

He turned uninterestedly to the paper's Bombay news page.

Killer Turned Mourner Held.

Some good police work done somewhere then.

It was like an Agatha Christie murder story. A mourner of the victim turning out to be the killer! . . . Within four hours the police arrested him on the charge of murdering his friend . . . According to police, Shripat went to Patya's house where both consumed liquor and slept. In the early hours Shripat woke up his friend as they had to go out for some work. This annoyed Patya. He assaulted Shripat with a stick which had an iron ring in the end.

Not a very difficult case by the sound of it. Only small fries involved. But someone had cleared it up promptly. And he himself was sitting here, suspended from duty, unable to clear up any case. Useless.

And a man dead just because of a fit of stupid anger caused by being in an alcoholic state. And Desai dead because of another fit of anger. Yet . . . Well, at the moment of decision in Vigatpore he had put himself squarely behind Tiger, and he did not regret that even now. Consequences regret, yes. But what he had done, no, no regret.

He was roused from this deep reverie by a change in the sound of the voices of the officers chatting amongst themselves.

He looked up.

S. M. Motabhoy had arrived, evidently with a story to tell.

'. . . unbolted the door and stepped out of the flat, and I thought I was still having that nightmare. People down at the bottom of the stairs screaming their heads off, servants everywhere in huddles wailing and whimpering. Little boys with raincoats over their nightclothes shrieking and laughing. Took me almost ten minutes down in the lobby to find out what was happening. Well, you know Sun Flower building where I stay, on Malabar Hill? Actually it is built in a hollow, and it turned out some retaining wall had broken under the pressure of flood water and the whole compound round was turned into a lake. You know what the weather was like last night.'

Ghote knew. The slapping pellets of rain had kept him awake hour after hour. That and the thoughts churning through his mind.

'Well,' S. M. Motabhoy went on, 'it was pretty dangerous. Petrol had leaked out of cars under water in the garages in the compound, and it was obvious that if anyone struck a match or if the water rose up as high as the electricity meters and caused a sparking the whole place could go up in flames. So panic set in, believe you me. There was a diamond merchant from the flat about us – he was a chap we knew just to wish hello in the mornings – and his wife was screaming at him to rescue her jewelleries, and, meek old Gujarati though he is, I thought he would turn on her and strangle her. And people were cursing the Fire Brigade because our calls were not answered. Ladies using language I never thought they were knowing. And all the time the water level was getting nearer and nearer those damn meters.'

'So what did you do, sir?' asked one of the junior officers.

'Took over the phone and got on to a chap I know at the B.E.S.T. and he got his engineers to cut off the current. Then at last a fire engine turned up and they pumped away enough water for it to be safe for us to evacuate. But I tell you I've ceased to think of the monsoon as fun any more. You know, going with the children for roasted bhutta on Marine Drive and watching the waves crashing over, and hot toddies and bowls of steaming soup. No, I suddenly felt sorry for all the hutments people soaking wet from monsoon start to monsoon finish and flooded out, too, as often as not, let alone the beggars who die from exposure.'

There was a murmur – sycophantic, Ghote thought – of appreciation.

S. M. Motabhoy looked round him.

'Well, sorry for the delay,' he said. 'But I think we should make a start now. Mr Sankar, you were going to call a fresh witness, wasn't it? Has he arrived all right? No rail lines cut?'

Ghote felt abruptly as if he had in a dream stepped over the edge of a precipice and was falling, falling.

In a few moments Shinde would be standing at the witness table, being asked about the night Desai had sent him out into the rain to buy a cigarette. What would he say? And if he produced the story he had been asked to tell, if he said that his hero, the new inspector, had not been in the station since before midnight, would he have the strength to repeat the lie again and again in the face of savage questioning?

The door was opened and the orderly brought Shinde in. He had made efforts, desperately obvious efforts, to look extra smart for the awesome occasion. His shirt, thin and much washed, had been ironed so ferociously that a crease stretched like a pencil line from one side of his chest to the other. His half-pants equally had been starched to board-like stiffness.

A few paces inside he came to a halt, thumped together his

heels, in wretched rubber chappals, and directed into the room in general his splay-fingered salute.

The orderly led him to the witness table.

R.K. was almost gentle as he took him through the preliminaries, his name, his position, his hours of duty.

'Now, I want you to think back to the night of June the 24th last year.'

'It is the night Desai Sergeant was drowned in the lake?'

R.K.'s eyes glittered frostily.

'Let us say it was the night when you last saw Sergeant Desai.'

'Achcha, sahib.'

'Now, tell us what happened in the police station from the time after the last man, except for the A.D.I.G. and Inspector Ghote, left duty.'

Shinde looked all round as if he expected to see some burly constable with a lathi waiting to beat him if he said anything unpleasing to the sahibs at the long table.

'Go on,' said R.K.

'It is about the cigarette?' Shinde asked.

'Well, we can begin there. You were requested by Sergeant Desai, who was still present though off duty, to go out, yes?'

'Ji, sahib.'

'At what time was this?'

'In the night, sahib.'

'Yes, yes. We know it was after dark. But I am asking at what time exactly you left the police station.'

'I am not knowing, sahib.'

'Come, man, you must have some idea. Was it at ten? At eleven? When?'

'Please, sahib, I am not able to tell the time.'

The R.K. pounced.

'And yet you told Inspector Sawant when he was making his inquiries – you remember Inspector Sawant? – that Inspector Ghote left the police station before midnight. I suggest to you, Shinde, that you can very well tell the time, and that you know very well at what hour it really was when Inspector Ghote left.'

But all this was plainly too complicated for the peon to follow. He shook his head in bewilderment and looked down at his feet in their battered rubber chappals.

R.K. drew in a slow breath and started again.

'Shinde, are you able to tell the time from a clock? Yes or no?'

'No, sahib.'

'But you told Inspector Sawant that Inspector Ghote left the police station before midnight, yes?'

'Yes, sahib. Inspectorji was leaving before-before midnight.'

'And how do you know that, Shinde? Was it because you looked at the clock you cannot read? Or was it because you were instructed to say that was the time at which Inspector Ghote left?'

Now it was out, fairly and squarely. Would Shinde, harassed as he was being, tell the truth now, unable to think of anything else?

He took a long time before replying, a big frown of puzzlement on his face.

'Sahib, it is this way. Some of the times in the clock I am able to tell. Time of *normal-end-of-duty*. Time at midday, two hands pointing up, up. Same also at midnight, though that I am not often seeing.'

'How very convenient,' R.K. said. 'And are there other times you can tell? Such as when you are due for your meal? When your officer takes his meal? And others? Are there? Answer me, please.'

'Yes, sahib. No, sahib.'

R.K. threw back his head.

'And what sort of answer is that? Yes and no. You are a very clever man, Shinde, to be able to answer both yes and no to the same question.'

'No, sahib. I am not at all clever. This is why I am Government Servant Class Four only.'

'But you still have not answered my question,' R.K. said, after the tiniest of pauses.

'Please, sahib, I am forgetting.'

'Forgetting what times you can tell, is it? Forgetting that you very well can tell any time you like? Forgetting that you told the time when you last saw Inspector Ghote that night, and that it was well after midnight?'

'No, sahib, no. Forgetting what is question.'

R.K. sighed.

'Very well. Will you please tell the Inquiry whether or not you can read the time from a clock. And this once, speak the truth.'

'Sahib, I have always spoken truth.'

And then poor Shinde pulled himself up short, and Ghote saw with plunging dismay that a dark blush was spreading up over his face.

It was as much as to say *Sahib, I have always spoken truth until Inspector Ghote begged me to lie for him.*

'You have always spoken the truth, have you, Shinde?' R.K. said, descending like a hooked-beak kite on to its prey. 'Then tell us the truth now. At what time did you last see Inspector Ghote on the night Sergeant Desai disappeared?'

There was a long, terrible silence. Ghote could see the peon's throat working as if there was a clotted lump there which he felt he must spit out or choke.

Then at last he managed to utter an answer.

'Sahib, before midnight.'

'You are telling us that Inspector Ghote left the police station before midnight? You are telling us that, though you have sworn to tell the truth?'

An almost childishly baffled look came on to Shinde's face then.

'Sahib?' he said.

'Yes, man, yes?'

'Sahib, when was I swearing to tell the truth?'

And Ghote realised, only just able to prevent a great smile breaking out, that Shinde in his simplicity had bested the great R.K. Because the fact of the matter was that, this not being a court of law, witnesses were not sworn. R.K., in close pursuit, had forgotten the circumstances, as he himself and even Mrs Ahmed had done earlier.

But R.K. was not the man to give way to fury, even after letting himself be caught out by a simple peon. With un-ruffled calm he resumed his questioning.

'Very well, you have not sworn. But I hope nevertheless you have some respect for the truth. And I am now going to ask you again to tell us, in truth, at what time Inspector Ghote left the police station at Vigatpore that night.'

'Sahib, before midnight.'

Shinde spoke the words with shining bravado.

Poor fellow, Ghote thought, little does he realise that with such an evident attitude he is almost saying aloud *I am telling a first-class lie*.

But plainly R.K. saw that there was no point in continuing to press his victim. That, if he did so, the brave lie would be repeated and repeated, and that in any case its falsity, if not wholly exposed, was more or less plain for everyone to see.

'Well, Shinde,' he said, 'we will pass over that "truth" you have chosen to put before us – for the moment.'

He gave a quick look towards the Board table to make doubly sure his point had got over. Then he turned back to the hapless peon.

'Let us instead look at some of the other things you did that night. For example, the cigarettes you went out to buy for Sergeant Desai.'

'No, sahib, I did not.'

'Not? Not? Now, we have had enough and more than enough of your lying. You told the Inquiry not ten minutes ago that you were sent by Desai to buy him cigarettes. Do you now dare to tell us this was not so?'

'Sahib, it was not so. One cigarette only Desai Sergeant sent me to buy.'

From the Board table there came, distinctly, the sound of an all but smothered laugh.

But once again R.K. showed no sign of being ruffled. Ghote, however, thought that he could detect beneath that air of glacial calm a yet harder determination to bring the victim to his knees.

Was there nothing he could do himself to intervene?

'One cigarette then, Shinde. I stand corrected. And at what hour did you leave to buy this one cigarette?'

'Sahib, I am not knowing. Only at my end-of-duty time and at midday and midnight also when the clock hands are the same as I am able to tell the time.'

'Are you attempting to say that you cannot give the court – give the Inquiry any idea of what time you left? Come, was it before the others in the station had been so conveniently sent out? Or after?'

But now Mrs Ahmed was on her feet, enraged. Or so to all appearances.

'Sir,' she addressed the Presiding Officer, 'this is monstrous. My client dismissed the personnel in the station that night solely on humanitarian grounds. To imply that he was sending them away for some nefarious purpose is wholly malafide.'

'Yes,' S. M. Motabhoy said benignly. 'I think perhaps that the last question should not go on the record.'

He looked across at the shorthand clerk's desk and waited until he had seen him draw a line through some symbols on his pad.

'Please continue, Mr Sankar,' he said.

R.K. gave a short melodramatic sigh and turned to Shinde again.

'Well now,' he said, 'cannot you give us any idea of when it was that you were sent out to buy that cigarette?'

Ghote know how important the repeated, trivial-seeming

question could be. If Shinde told the Inquiry when he had left the station, and if R.K. was then able to establish that he had been away for some considerable time, it could become clear that Shinde had not been present at about half-past eleven, and his earlier lie would be exposed. But Shinde, God bless him, was hardly likely to be able to work this out.

He waited with sharp trepidation for the reply.

'Sahib, it was raining when I was leaving.'

'Ah.'

R.K. pounced again.

'Now, at what time did the rain start and finish that night? And let me warn you, Shinde, that if necessary other evidence can be brought on this matter. Now, tell the Inquiry: when did the rain start?'

'Sahib, it was starting just when darkness came.'

'Good. That has the ring of a truthful answer. At last. Now, when did the rain cease?'

This was the crucial moment, Ghote thought. The rain – how vividly he could recall it – had slackened to not much more than a drizzle while he and Tiger had been wheeling that slumped body through the outskirts of the town. If Shinde indicated that he had got back from buying Desai's cigarette after the rain had eased off then it would be clear that he himself had been at the station to say goodnight to him and leave at a much later time than 11.30. And there would be scientific evidence from the Weather Bureau at Colaba to establish the time the rain had lessened.

But again this was hardly something which a Class Four Government Servant could be expected to work out.

Yet it was plain, at least to him, that Shinde was attempting to do the sum. Would he arrive at an answer that was consistent with the lie he had been persuaded to tell and had stuck to so loyally?

'Sahib . . .' Shinde said at last, with horrible hesitancy.

'The time the rain ceased or slackened?' R.K. demanded.

'Oh, sahib, by then I was so wet I was not at all able to tell whether it was hard-hard rain or soft only.'

R.K. simply turned to the Board and lifted eloquent shoulders.

'Well,' he said with calmness, ominous calmness, 'let us try to get at this vexed question by another route.'

He turned again to Shinde, who produced for him a tentative, uncomprehending smile.

'At what hour did you yourself reach your quarter that night?'

'Oh, sahib, I am not knowing.'

'Of course not. But you have a wife, have you?'

'Oh, yes, sahib. Very good wife.'

'I trust, Shinde, we shall not have to call this wife of yours from Vigatpore to Bombay, to call her into this very room, to ask her the questions which you seem so singularly unable to provide us with answers to.'

'Please, sahib?'

'Do you want your wife to stand where you are now?'

'Oh, no, sahib. That would not be very good at all. She is very fearful and she is not understanding anything also. Not like me, sahib.'

'Well then, will you try to understand this, and give us an answer in which we can all believe? At what time did you reach your quarter that night?'

'Sahib, it is hard to say.'

'It is not. You must have known when you got there. Now, tell us the exact truth.'

'Please, sahib?'

Into Shinde's eyes there had come the expression that enters a dog's when it is given a command beyond its comprehension.

'Answer, man. At what time did you reach your quarter?'

'Sahib, I cannot.'

Ghote, pinned to his hard little chair, felt for the fellow.

Once more he was having to find a second lie to back up

the first. If he truly told them the time he had got back home, the whole game would be given away in an instant. If he failed to provide a satisfactory answer, his wife would be hauled from Vigatpore, be subjected to R.K.'s attacks, and in all probability state the actual simple truth.

He felt a desire, from deep within himself, to leap to his feet, to shout out *Yes, yes, I did help Tiger Kelkar all the time, and I asked this poor fellow to lie for me. And he has done it. But now, now, you have the truth.*

He grasped the sides of his chair with both hands, as if physically to prevent himself rising. And he swore that he would not let Shinde endure this torment beyond just one question more.

'Come, this is arrant nonsense. It is plain to us, to every single person in this room, that you are prevaricating. Now, stop that altogether. Answer my question, and answer with the truth. At what time did you yourself reach your quarter?'

'Sahib, my wife was sleeping-sleeping when I was reaching. My three-four children also. Sahib, it must have been before the time the clock hands were pointing up-up.'

'Before midnight?'

'Yes, sahib, before midnight. I am saying.'

R. K. Sankar sank down on to his chair and waved the witness away.

14

Once more Ghote made his way on his phut-phutting old scooter back home for a midday meal. Doing so left him little time, in fact, to eat. But he felt that if he took any tiffin anywhere near the Old Secretariat he might see someone else involved in the Inquiry, if only the shorthand writer or the stout old long-service havildar who acted as receptionist at the entrance. And he wanted for a few minutes at least to get away from all the menace that hung over him.

Certainly the journey made forgetting that easy. Weaving through the traffic with the rain steadily descending making the roads stream with water two or three inches deep at times, effectively prevented him from thinking of anything except keeping his machine upright. Potholes, where the slapdash repairs of the previous year had been washed out, were another hazard. As were the pedestrians who, blinded by rain and their inevitable umbrellas, made wild darts from one side of the road to the other.

A girl did that now, one hand holding a wildly swaying coloured umbrella, the other hoisting up her sari, the red dye of her forehead kum-kum running in a trickle down the centre of her nose. He wobbled violently but managed to keep his machine going and get round behind her. But all too soon he was forced to a halt as the traffic in front came, vehicle by vehicle, to a solid jammed mass.

Another waterlogging, he thought. Or perhaps trouble with some handcart loaded with three or four old chairs to ferry people over a deeper flood. They were always getting stuck and producing outbreaks of shouting, illegal horning and more bad temper than that brought on by the perpetual damp and the hordes of new-bred mosquitoes.

He waited with some patience.

What new witness would R.K. bring in this afternoon? And who was it who was helping him prepare the terrible case he was putting?

He shook the anxious pricklings from his mind.

On the Fiat immediately in front of him he saw a rat, driven out by flood water, take a frenzied leap off a piece of half-sunken wood in a puddle and on to the car's rear bumper. It scampered across and dived off on the far side. A twinge of unaccustomed pity moved him. He too knew what it was to be harassed by unknown forces from unknown directions.

The Fiat started forward and he set off again.

Home at last, Protima had food ready for him. And questions.

He knew she had a right to hear how the morning had gone, but he longed not to have to tell her. Poor Shinde had managed to maintain his lie, however obvious it was that he had been lying. But to explain it all to Protima, to live those fears all over again: he shrank from it.

So, as he slipped into the pair of fresh socks she had warmed for him by the stove in the kitchen, he began instead quickly to tell her the tale of S. M. Motabhoy's adventure of the night before.

He laid it on a bit describing, as S. M. Motabhoy hardly had, the water rising inch by inch with its dangerous floating layer of petrol.

'And what happened? What happened?' Protima demanded.

Then, without waiting for his reply, she flew into a spat of rage.

'Oh, why you can never tell me anything properly? Why must you go through it all from start to finish, one, two, three, as if you were telling a judge or a magistrate only? Did it all catch fire? Were people charred to death? Tell me. Tell me.'

'I have told already that S. M. Motabhoy was arriving at the Inquiry,' Ghote snapped back. 'You must see from that how it was all okay in the end.'

'Well then, if it was, why were you making so much of a story?'

Ghote almost replied *Just to stop you eating my head about the damned Inquiry*. But he stopped himself in time. He owed Protima that and much more. The least he could do was to stand back from a pointless quarrel.

Instead he said the first thing that came into his head.

'You know, I am thinking that Motabhoy Sahib is not so much of a rotten fellow as I was believing.'

'But you never told me you were believing that,' Protima answered. 'Why do you never tell anything about the Inquiry? Is S. M. Motabhoy full of bad thoughts towards you? Will he bring in guilty verdict despite the evidences?'

Ghote sighed.

'There will not be any verdict whatsoever,' he said. 'I have explained. What will happen in the end is, if I am found to have been derelict in my duty, the Presiding Officer will issue a Show Cause notice stating what punishment is proposed. That is all.'

'But you will not be found – what is that word? – derelict. You cannot be.'

'But I can be,' Ghote said. 'I was. You know it.'

'But no one but you only can know truly what you did for Kelkar Sahib that night. So unless you are telling, they

139

cannot find you derelict. Except for S. M. Motabhoy not acting on what he has heard.'

'Well,' Ghote said peaceably, 'you will not have much to fear then. I begin to think S. M. Motabhoy is a first-class chap after all. He acted very well at his flats block, insisting to get the current shut down. Just as Tiger would have done. And at the Inquiry also he is very much seeing fair play.'

But soon it was time for him to wrap himself again in his plastic cape, wriggle into his gumboots and go out and crouch over his scooter, hoping in a self-induced panic that the damp would not prevent it starting.

He made the return journey, with the moist air wetting his face although the rain itself had eased off, without mishap. To find, when the sitting was resumed, that R.K. was calling as his next witness the single remaining servant from Shivram Patel's big, echoingly empty house at Vigatpore.

Would the ruse which Tiger had barked an order at him to adopt, there in the dark by the lake shore that night, prove to have worked? When, having crossed that neglected, perhaps snake-infested compound, he had woken the old servant, had the fellow been sleepy enough to have believed the time was 'almost midnight'?

There must, in fact, be some uncertainty about it in his mind. Otherwise the person who had prepared R.K.'s case, whoever that was, would not have suggested calling him. But equally the old man – he came grouchily into the room at that moment, bent with his years of hard work, a silver grey stubble on his lean face – could not possibly have been sure of the real time that night or he would have contradicted his own statement there and then.

'So on this night of June 24th,' R.K. was soon asking, 'or to be more correct in the early hours of June the 25th, you were woken from sleep by a knocking at the door of the house?'

'A tapping and tapping with the door chain, yes, sahib. It was so.'

'And you went and unbarred the door and there found Inspector Ghote?'

'Yes, it was so.'

'Now, can you tell us at what hour this was?'

The old man took his time over his answer.

'Sahib, it was in the night. I do not have a clock.'

'But you are able to tell the time from a clock?'

'Oh, yes, sahib, that I am well able to do.'

'But on your way to open the door, was there no clock you happened to see?'

'Sahib, it was very dark. I am having to light a lantern before I could go down to the door. We are no more having electricity.'

'Very well. And I presume you do not have a watch?'

'That is so, sahib.'

'But nevertheless if at night something should chance to wake you, if perhaps you suffered from some stomach pain, you would have some idea how much of the night had passed?'

'Yes, sahib. When I catch the whistle of the night train or when in monsoon time there is much thunder and I sometimes wake, I know whether it is just only the start of the night or whether morning is not far away.'

'Good. Excellent. So now can you tell us how much of the night had passed before you unbarred the door for Inspector Ghote?'

The old man shook his head from side to side in slow puzzlement.

'Sahib, it is difficult. I had the feeling that much, much of the night had gone. But Inspector Sahib was saying it is only almost midnight.'

Ghote found he was holding his breath hard, and did his best to let it out in silence.

'Inspector Ghote told you that the hour was "almost midnight"?' R.K. asked, his voice quiet as a cat creeping towards a bird.

141

'Yes, sahib. As I have said.'

'But you, used to knowing without benefit of clock or watch how much of the night had passed, you believed that it was very much later.'

'Sahib, I did.'

'So perhaps it was that Inspector Ghote was endeavouring to trick you into believing something that was not the truth?'

But, before the slow speaking old man could begin to answer, Mrs Ahmed was on her feet, blazing anger in every inch of her sober sari-clad frame.

'Mr Presiding Officer, such a question is grossly improper. Mr Sankar is attempting to elicit opinion from a witness with no technical competence whatever.'

'Well, yes,' S. M. Motabhoy said. 'I think I must agree.'

He looked across at the witness table with a kindly air.

'That is something you do not have to answer,' he said.

R.K. was undismayed. Palpably.

'Then there is nothing further I wish to ask,' he said.

'But there is a great deal I would like to ask,' Mrs Ahmed retorted, still with anger crackling in her voice.

Ghote, despite his anxiety over what R.K. had got the old servant to say, wondered briefly how much of that anger was genuine. Certainly as an advocate Mrs Ahmed had a duty to appear angry when her client's reputation was maligned. But was she only like a country actor making terrible faces in imitation of the rudra rasa, the furious temper? Only putting on a show? Yet her fury did really seem to be the true thing. Perhaps it was that her anger – the long-growing fruit of that first great injustice of her life, her little brother's banishment – lay close to the surface. A similar anger had done with Tiger. And in her case the least hint of an injustice or an untruth brought it up, boiling and spilling over.

But now how was she going to put right what R.K. had contrived to put wrong? Only, R.K. had not put it wrong. He had extracted from the old man with his shreds of dignity what was after all nothing less than the simple truth. And

Mrs Ahmed, fighter for truth, was there on his own behalf to reverse that declaration.

She looked at the old man in silence for some moments. Then she spoke, quietly and with evident seriousness.

'Tell me, do you know how much depends for Inspector Ghote on what you say to the Inquiry?'

'What is depending . . . ?'

'I see that you do not. So let me explain before I ask you anything more. Then you will answer after giving your replies proper thought. Do you understand, then, that if what you have said is true beyond doubt and Inspector Ghote did not arrive at your master's house until long after midnight, then the Inspector's account of what he did that night will be seen as false? And that he will be in danger of being dismissed as a police officer, dismissed after many years of good service, of upholding the law, of securing justice for the victims of wrongdoers?'

As she delivered each of these hammer strokes – and as Ghote flinched internally at each one – it was plain that they were having their effect, one by one, on the old man. The look of burdened responsibility on his face grew and grew.

'Do you understand that?'

'Yes. Yes, Now I am understanding.'

The old servant looked across at Ghote as if he was seeing an object of fearful worth, the most precious possession his master had owned before the loss of his fortune which with the dusting cloth he habitually carried across his shoulder he might at any moment send crashing from its place.

'Now,' said Mrs Ahmed, 'think carefully before you reply. At such times as you have woken in the night before, were you always without fail correct in your guessing what time it was?'

The old man's hand went to the stubble at his chin and caressed it apprehensively.

'Now, think,' Mrs Ahmed repeated. 'And answer.'

'Perhaps not, not every single time. I cannot remember.'

'Perhaps not every single time, I see. So, now will you tell us again what time you thought it was when you opened the house door to Inspector Ghote on the night of June the 24th last year?'

'I do not know. He was saying it was before midnight. It may have been so. I am an old man. Sometimes I make mistakes.'

'You have done well, very well, to admit as much before these sahibs,' Mrs Ahmed concluded.

And down she sat.

R.K. did not appear to be put out by this defeat. If anything, Ghote thought with a shrilling of alarm, his features betrayed a gleam of unaccountable pleasure.

In a moment it began to become evident why this might be.

'With your concurrence, Mr Presiding Officer,' R.K. said, 'I think there should still be time this afternoon to hear one more witness, one less subject to confusion than the last.'

S. M. Motabhoy consulted his watch.

'Yes, Mr Sankar, unless you expect to be very long, we should have time enough.'

'Oh, I do not think I shall require much time,' R.K. said. 'I may need in essence to ask my witness one question only.'

'Very well then. Who is it you wish to call?'

'It is Shri Shivram Patel, owner of the house we have just been concerned with.'

15

Why should R.K. be calling the boar-like, defeated former owner of the creamery near Vigatpore? Ghote asked himself with jabbing anxiety. Shivram Patel had, surely, been asleep at the far end of his big old house at the late hour he himself had summoned the servant to the door and tricked him, more or less, into thinking it was before midnight.

So why was R.K. producing his master as a witness?

The door was pushed open and Shivram Patel himself entered, heavy of tread, sullen looking, dressed in perhaps the last of the finery left to him since he had ceased being able to exploit the peasants who had brought milk to his creamery. On his head was a cap of embroidered velvet. His bulky frame was hidden by a silk Lucknow kurta in a shade of pale pink. In his hand he carried an ebony cane, topped with silver.

Guided by the orderly he moved with slow ponderousness to the witness table and R.K. put him through the preliminaries.

'And now, Mr Patel, we come to the night of June the 24th last year, or, as I have said before, to the early hours of June the 25th.'

Mrs Ahmed was on her feet, taut with anger, in an instant.

'Mr Presiding Officer, on the previous occasion Mr Sankar made that assumption, which is clean contrary to my client's account of the events of that night, I let it pass. But I cannot do so a second time. Will you direct that both his remarks be taken off the record?'

S. M. Motabhoy gave the point a few moments' consideration.

'Yes,' he said, 'I think we cannot in justice allow either remark.'

He turned to the shorthand clerk.

'Can you find the previous instance Mrs Ahmed referred to? It must have been at the start of the evidence of the last witness.'

The clerk riffled wildly through his notebook and at last said he had found the words. S. M. Motabhoy watched him cross them out.

'Now, Mr Sankar, you may resume.'

'Thank you, sir.'

R.K. turned to Shivram Patel again.

'We come now, shall we say, to the night in question. You understand to what I am referring?'

'Oh, yes. To when the inspector from Bombay was so late out. To the first night of the monsoon last year.'

'Exactly. Now, will you tell us what happened of your own knowledge that night?'

'Yes.'

The boar-like owner of the house where on his prickly straw mattress Ghote had slept so badly took some moments to think. The eyes, deep-sunk in his well-fleshed face, shone with the malevolency Ghote well remembered from their acquaintance a year and more before.

'That night the thunder was often waking me,' he began at last. 'But then a different noise woke me once more. Someone beating and knocking at the door of the house. I heard my servant, the only servant I have remaining from a house that was once full of servants, get up and go and see who was so shameless to be making so much of noise, and for some reason I also got up from my bed. By the time I had done so my man had lit a lamp and was going down to the door. By the last of its light I followed. But I did not go so far as the door itself. Instead I waited and watched from some distance. And at last I saw that the person who had made all the noise was the inspector, the inspector I had been forced to take into my home.'

Ghote listened to this unfolding tale with a growing sense of sick defeat. R.K. and his unknown investigator had tricked him and Mrs Ahmed with utter cunning. Shivram Patel's servant had been allowed to say he believed the time he had been woken was before midnight and that this was because of what he himself had said. And all the while his actual arrival had been watched by the master of the house. No doubt in answer to the next question Shivram Patel would state he had noted the time his night's sleep had been interrupted.

So now the alibi he had thought secure had not only been broken but had been shown to have been concocted deliberately and to have been persisted with since. Now R.K. would be able to show, with evidence, that it had been at about 3 a.m. that he had come in, and that therefore that whole account of his actions which till now had been only a guessed-at reconstruction was in all likelihood the actual truth.

As it was. As it was.

'Now, Mr Patel, are you able to tell the Inquiry at what time this occurred?'

'Yes, that I can do most definitely. To the minute even.'

'Good. And why is that?'

'Because when I was standing seeing my servant allow in the inspector I was also at the same time seeing a clock.'

'Ah. There is a clock in your house somewhere near the door?'

'Yes, yes. For many years it has been there. My father

147

before me built the house and he was also buying the clock. A very fine timepiece.'

'A clock, we can take it then, that keeps good time?'

'Never does it lose, never does it gain.'

'Excellent. So, now: at what time was it by this notable timepiece that Inspector Ghote entered your house?'

Shivram Patel turned and gave Ghote, upright on his hard chair, a glare of rich hatred.

'The time the inspector was returning was at ten minutes before three o'clock in the morning,' he said.

Ghote felt the words, expecting them though he had been, as a side-hand chop to the back of his neck.

But almost simultaneously with their impact there came into his head a clear visual memory of his first arrival at the old house. He saw the servant with his soot-smeared hurricane lamp held high. He saw the bare, empty rooms he had been led past. He saw the places on the plaster walls where evidently pieces of furniture had stood for years before they had been sold.

And he saw an unmistakable round shape high up on a wall near the entrance hall. The shape of a big old round clock.

He turned and whispered urgently to Mrs Ahmed.

She nodded, then rose for her cross-examination.

'Mr Patel, I am interested in this clock which you have described with such loving care. It was bought by your father, you say?'

'Yes. My father was buying it on a visit to Bombay, from Army and Navy Stores, a top-notch British shop. In those days there was nothing like that clock in the whole district.'

'And it has always kept, you said, excellent time?'

'Not one minute slow, not one minute fast. Never.'

'Mr Patel, am I right in understanding that some years ago you suffered a financial reverse?'

Shivram Patel's deep-sunk eyes glowed in fury.

'The cobras and sons of cobras,' he stormed. 'Their dirty

machinations were depriving me of everything. What for did they want dairy cooperative? Was I not always buying milk from those casteless swine? Was I not always giving them a good price?'

'Perhaps you were, Mr Patel. But nevertheless a cooperative was established and very soon not a single peasant was bringing milk to your creamery. Am I right?'

'It was a most vile injustice. Vile. Vile.'

'But it occurred?'

'Yes.'

'And in consequence you have had to sell a great many of your possessions? Of your possessions and the possessions you inherited from your father?'

And at last Shivram Patel's hatred for all the world and all around him was pierced by the realisation of what the questions he had been asked were leading to. He looked wildly from side to side.

'No. Yes. Some things I was selling, yes,' he answered at last.

'Among them the clock that had hung in its place so long that you were unable to imagine that wall without it being there?'

'No.'

'Mr Patel, let me remind you that this is a matter which we can easily find witnesses to prove. Now, did you or did you not sell that clock long before Inspector Ghote came to your house as a paying guest?'

A long silence.

Then, his face darkening, Shivram Patel answered.

'It was sold.'

After that R.K. did not attempt to retrieve an impossible position.

Ghote, watching the dispossessed creamery owner shamble out, sat back in his hard chair as if in the greatest of cushioned ease. He had escaped. He had, thanks to that flash of memory, been delivered from Shivram

Patel's monstrous lie. A falsehood that would have been crushing.

Yet that lie – he jerked upright again, all feelings of cushioned comfort gone – had in fact backed up what was no less than the truth. It had been, in truth, at about three in the morning that he had arrived at the house that night, hastily traversing the snake-dangerous compound, and, yes, tapping rather than beating and knocking at the door.

But evidently S. M. Motabhoy had also been considering the matter of the lie and how it had come to be told. Because, leaning forward now, he addressed the two advocates.

'Mr Sankar, Mrs Ahmed, I feel that in the interests of a fully just hearing we ought to be appraised before we proceed any further of the exact circumstances which caused this last witness to present evidence so palpably false. I suggest the best way we can achieve this is for the officer who investigated the implications of the late A.D.I.G. Kelkar's dying statement to come to the witness table and answer such questions as you, Mrs Ahmed, may like to put.'

R.K. gave a deep shrug of his thin shoulders under the long black atchkan.

'I cannot, of course, have any objection, Mr Presiding Officer.'

'Very well then,' S. M. Motabhoy said.

He turned to the Inquiry orderly.

'I imagine Inspector Pimputkar is in the building,' he said. 'Will you bring him as soon as possible?'

Inspector Pimputkar.

So he, Ghote thought, has been the man who has prepared the case against me.

Pimputkar was an officer feared, loathed even, throughout the State force. He was the chief investigator for Vigilance Branch at the force headquarters in Pune. As such his task was to inquire into allegations or suspicions of corruption. It was a duty which ought not to seem odious. But Pimputkar, notoriously, took pleasure in his task. Officers who had had to answer his questions, even when they were not in any way implicated in a particular investigation, had tales to tell that sent tremors of disquiet through the minds of even the most honest. Pimputkar, they said, brought to his questioning a fury of suspiciousness which made even innocent actions look devious.

No wonder that opening statement of R.K.'s had seemed almost as if he had been hovering over Vigatpore that night, peering through the heavy rain-weeping monsoon cloud, watching every move he and Tiger had made. It had not been R.K. who had been there then: it had been Pimputkar prying and suggesting afterwards.

It took the orderly some little time to locate this un-expectedly summoned witness. The officers of the Board began chatting quietly. R.K., behind his table with its impressive piles of papers, leant back in his solid wooden-armed chair and closed his eyes with a tremendous show of weariness. Mrs Ahmed soon delved into her bulging bag and produced a document, typed in purple, evidently referring to some injustice she was concerned with. Ghote could hear, as she perused it, little sighs and puffs of wrathfulness.

But he himself sat in stone-like silence, sunk beneath flood waters of depression. Stories of Pimputkar's triumphs, vague in outline but frightening for the odd details that floated into his mind, oppressed him. The man was a mongoose, sharp-teethed, glittering-eyed, intent on his prey. And the fact that such prey was always, in theory at least, some sort of evil snake did nothing to soften the image that had come into his head.

So that, when at last the orderly opened the door and stood aside for Pimputkar himself to enter, the sight of his pursuer – he had never till this moment set eyes on him, for all the talk he had heard in canteen conversations and long night waits – came as an anticlimax.

He was a man of remarkably average appearance, neither particularly large – at one moment he had expected to see a towering ogre – nor noticeably small, for all that a rat-like creature had been another image he had built up. All that at all distinguished him was that he was thin in the face. Its flesh might, indeed, have been eaten away by some consuming internal fire.

He marched stiffly across to the witness table and stood at attention behind it.

Mrs Ahmed put to him the statutory questions about his name and rank and the authority for his investigation. He answered each with snapped-off precision, as if that inner fire was preventing him parting with one single piece of information not properly demanded of him.

At least, after what had seemed to Ghote an interminable time, Mrs Ahmed came to the matter over which Pimputkar had been brought in. At her request the shorthand writer turned back to the last few answers Shivram Patel had given and read them out. Falteringly and with several abysmal mispronunciations he stumbled his way to that final betraying *It was sold*.

'Now, Inspector,' Mrs Ahmed said, 'that witness, Shri Shivram Patel, was brought to give evidence as a result of your inquiries?'

'Yes.'

'You realise that what he first told us was no more than mere malicious invention?'

'Yes.'

'Can you account to the Inquiry for what reason you were deceived by this man's wanton lies?'

'He offered a statement corroborating what his servant had told me. I accepted it.'

'You were anxious to accept any evidence that would seem to tell against Inspector Ghote?'

Pimputkar's eyes glittered momentarily with suppressed fury. But he did not let any of it emerge in words.

'No.'

'You chose to believe the servant's doubtful notion that it

152

might have been 3 a.m. and not midnight when he let Inspector Ghote in?'

'Yes.'

'It did not occur to you that Inspector Ghote's statement as to the time would be more likely?'

'No.'

A moment of hesitation. And then an addition.

'I continue to trust the expressed belief of the servant.'

Mrs Ahmed looked quickly down at her desk. Such a firmly delivered statement would hardly benefit her case.

'Well,' she said, 'you were not brought here this afternoon to do anything other than explain why it was that you believed the lies Mr Shivram Patel put before us.'

But R.K., for all that he had continued to lean back in his chair with eyes closed, was not going to let such a chance go by. He was on his feet in a moment.

'Mr Presiding Officer, it would seem to me convenient, since we have Inspector Pimputkar with us, to pursue this line at the present time. Might I put some questions?'

S. M. Motabhoy took his customary second or two for consideration.

'Yes,' he said then. 'I agree, Mr Sankar. I think we should hear from Inspector Pimputkar why he continues to believe one impression about that time rather than another.'

Ghote sat looking from Pimputkar to R.K. and back again. He felt abruptly now that the whole invention he had embarked on with Tiger's backing, and which he had promised Protima he would stand by, was no more than a frail leaning fence of pieces of rusted corrugated iron patched with rotting gunny strips. Before the whistling wind which these two pursuers would sweep down at it the whole wretched screen would be sent whirling away in a moment.

16

R.K. gave a little tug to the sides of his long atchkan.
It indicated somehow a fresh start, and Ghote, sweaty-
thighed on his hard chair, experienced a new interior
qualm.

'Now, Inspector Pimputkar, we have disposed, quite satis-
factorily to my mind, of the unfortunate matter of the
evidence given by Shri Shivram Patel, and we come to the
evidence, the more impressive evidence, of Shri Patel's
servant, the man who actually admitted Inspector Ghote to
the house on that fatal night.'

'Yes, sir,' Pimputkar said, with a little, licking trace of
excitement.

'Now, in the course of your investigations you asked this
man a simple question: at what hour did Inspector Ghote
knock at the house door?'

'Yes, sir.'

'And what answer did he give?'

'He stated that it was at approximately three ack emma.'

'Three o'clock in the morning, I see. And did you have any
reason to doubt that statement?'

'No, sir. It was his other statement that I felt to be
doubtful.'

'His other statement? What statement was this, Inspector?'

'That Inspector Ghote had complained to him that he had been kept waiting at the door "at almost midnight".'

'At almost midnight? The man distinctly recounted to you that this was what Inspector Ghote had said? That he had been told in so many words that it was "almost midnight"?'

'Yes, sir.'

'And you thought this was – shall we say – curious?'

'I did, sir. I saw no reason why a person arriving at a house and needing to have the door unbarred for him should state what time it was.'

'No. No, that I can understand. So what conclusion did you draw, Inspector?'

'I considered that this statement as to the hour was in the nature of a trick, sir.'

'A trick?'

'Yes, sir. Intended to confuse an ignorant and aged man as to the correct hour.'

'I see. Yes. And in such further questioning as you saw fit to put there was nothing that caused you to alter that opinion?'

'No, sir.'

'I see. Well, I think that is all we need to know, Inspector.'

But, of course, Mrs Ahmed was on her feet almost before R.K. had finished his dismissive conclusion.

'Mr Presiding Officer, there is a great deal more that we are needing to know.'

'Then kindly put such questions as you may have, Mrs Ahmed.'

Ghote's belief in his defender grew to a new height in the next quarter of an hour. She was unable to make Pimputkar retract his reliance on the old servant's estimate of the time as being about 3 a.m. But by harping again and again on such weak points as his not seeing how likely it was that anyone kept waiting so late should mention the time, and by other occasional asides indicating her own opinion of Pimputkar as a prejudiced witness she did a considerable amount to put his testimony in doubt.

Yes, he was lucky to have found Mrs Ahmed. She would not stand back from the fight.

Even though – his heart shrank – unknown to herself she was fighting in an unjust cause.

'Very well,' S. M. Motabhoy said, when she indicated she had no further questions, 'you may stand down, Inspector Pimputkar. But I should warn you to hold yourself in readiness. The Inquiry will wish to hear further from you.'

Ghote watched Pimputkar march smartly from the room. And he wished with all his might that this could be the last he would see of him. But S. M. Motabhoy's words were still in his ears. *The Inquiry will wish to hear further from you.*

R.K. came to his feet again.

'I should like now, with your permission, Mr Presiding Officer, to bring before the Inquiry one Vasantrao Chavan.'

'Yes, Mr Sankar. We have plenty of time. Proceed.'

Now, who was it that R.K. was summoning up, Ghote asked himself. The name meant nothing to him, but it was a common enough one in parts of Maharashtra. Yet who could R.K. and Pimputkar in the cat-and-mouse game they were playing with him be going to produce next? Thanks to the lines on which S. M. Motabhoy had said the Inquiry was to be conducted, the two of them had been able to bring forward witnesses in whatever order they pleased and had contrived to do so in a way best calculated to blast down his defences as each one of them was erected.

So why were they bringing in this Balvantrao Chavan? No, Vasantrao Chavan. Could he come from Vigatpore? Certainly he could not be anybody who had actually seen himself and Tiger with Desai's drooping body on that bicycle.

The night, when they had set out, had been far too tumultuously rainy for anyone to have ventured out of doors except for the most urgent reasons. And, surely, in sleepy Vigatpore there were no urgent reasons.

He clung on to this last thought.

It was the key to his whole scheme of lies. The lies on which all his future depended. The lies which, battered but still intact, stood between a life of wretchedness and misery and the taking up once again of the life he was meant to lead. His karma, if Pandit Balkrishan was to be taken at his word.

He shifted in his chair to get a better view of the tall door of the room. But there was no sign of it opening, no sounds from outside of steps banging down, echoing out.

Mrs Ahmed was deep, once again, in the purple typed document she had taken up when they had had to wait for Pimputkar to appear. It consisted of a good many pages, and he could imagine the heart's-core effort that had, long ago, gone into producing it. R.K. had resumed his attitude of apparent sleep. The members of the Board had begun to chat again, talking no doubt about every sort of triviality, the price hike in rainwear, where the deepest flood in the city was to be found, the latest film, their wives' latest holyman and how he had spotted out her symptoms straight away.

Then, at last, there came the sound of steps in the corridor, the slap of the orderly's heavy regulation chappals. And what other sound? Something hard to make out. Bare feet. Yes, bare feet, most probably.

So who? Who was it R.K. was calling? This Vasantrao, no Balvantrao, no Vasantrao Chavan?

He looked across at R.K. His eyes were just not closed, two glinting slits.

The door opened and the orderly ushered in a wide-eyed man who obviously held some menial job somewhere. Barefooted, yes, with a pair of khaki half-pants above thin knobbly knees and a well-washed, faded shirt that had once had a gay pattern of small yellow aircraft on it.

The orderly directed him, almost manhandled him, to the witness table. The officers of the Board turned away from

each other and assumed alert and interested expressions.
S. M. Motabhoy gave a small beneficient nod to R.K.

R.K. got to his feet.

'You are Vasantrao Chavan?'

The man at the witness table looked round the big room
like a scared rabbit and at last located who it had been who
had demanded his name.

'You are Vasantrao Chavan?' R.K. repeated wearily.

'Yes. Yes, sahib. That is being my name.'

Vasantrao Chavan looked at once as if he feared it had
been the greatest mistake to have admitted this.

R.K. sighed.

'You are by occupation a dhobi?'

A dhobi, Ghote thought. Why should Pimputkar have dug
up a washerman to give evidence? What was he going to give
evidence of?

'Ji, sahib. I am dhobi.'

'One of the places where you go to collect clothes for
washing is the residence of Mrs G. V. Ghote?'

Ghote did not hear the dhobi's reply. His mind was too full
of a wild flux of anger and appalled dismay.

Pimputkar, that biting mongoose, had penetrated to the
very heart of his existence. To his own home. Somehow he
felt now that, whatever evidence the dhobi was to give,
it must betray him entirely. If Pimputkar's claws had
reached this far into his life, what would he not have found
out?

The man might have been crouching somewhere just
outside the open window when he had first confessed to
Protima what had actually happened on that fearful night in
Vigatpore.

Sitting on his hard chair in the high-ceilinged room, he
shook his head in sharp self-reproof.

What nonsense he had let himself think. That window at
home was far too high for any eavesdropper. But Ved, young
Ved, might not Pimputkar somehow have got hold of him?

No, again that was nonsense. The boy knew nothing. He might, in fact, have been wondering what had been happening in their little world. He was old enough to have his suspicions of the story about extra casual leave he had been given to account for those long days of idleness. But he had been told not a word of the true state of affairs, so there was nothing Pimputkar could find out from him.

But, all the same, the very thought of the fellow making inquiries round about his home, even to questioning the dhobi and discovering – Discovering what?

He forced himself to pay attention to R.K. again.

'Now, can you remember a particular day rather more than a year ago, during the early monsoon, when you collected from Mrs Ghote an unusual piece of dirty washing?'

The dhobi grasped the table edge in front of him and leant forward, twisting his head to look at R.K. with a tremendous air of being willing to cooperate.

'This is what that Inspector Sahib was telling?' he asked.

Mrs Ahmed was up in an instant.

'Mr Presiding Officer, this witness has clearly been instructed in his testimony.'

But R.K. was undismayed.

'Mr Presiding Officer, this Inquiry has been convened, in your own words if I recollect them, to elicit the truth of the events of June the 24th and 25th last year. We have before us a dhobi who spends his life collecting and washing dirty clothes of all varieties from a considerable number of persons. How is he to recall a particular transaction more than a year ago unless he is to some degree prompted?'

S. M. Motabhoy considered. And then pronounced.

'Yes, I see no way we can get to the heart of this matter without some such instruction of the witness. Proceed, Mr Sankar.'

'Thank you, sir.'

R.K. turned to the dhobi once more.

'Yes,' he said, 'we are talking about the time which Inspector Pimputkar asked you about. The time during the last monsoon when you collected from Mrs Ghote certain items for washing. Will you tell us, please, what they were?'

The dhobi clasped his hands together in his eagerness to produce the wanted answer.

'Oh, yes, sahib. It was as that Inspector Sahib was telling. Two pieces of police officer uniform.'

Ghote looked behind him at Mrs Ahmed. Should she not be protesting again against such prompted evidence?

But wearily she shook her head in negative, as much as to say there was no point if S. M. Motabhoy was determined to conduct the Inquiry in the way he was.

And Ghote, turning back to look at the too willing witness once more – what threats had Pimputkar used? – realised just how seriously the fellow could damage his case. What was in question, no doubt, was the uniform he had been wearing on that appalling night. With his temporary assignment ending so abruptly he had had no time in Vigatpore to get it washed there and so he had brought it back to Bombay terribly mud-stained. How could he account for that? What could he say to Mrs Ahmed, so that she would have counter-questions to put to this wretched dhobi?

Or was this the moment when he would have to tell her the truth after all? And if he did, what would she say to him, this true champion of good causes?

'Do you know whose uniform this was?' R.K. was asking now.

'Oh, yes, sahib. Inspector uniform. The three stars on the shoulder had been taken off because when you beat the clothes they get beaten also. But I could see the marks where they had been.'

'You are most observant. So, tell us, what else did you notice about this uniform?'

'Very very dirty, sahib. Pant most dirty. Very much of mud.'

Ghote's mind raced.

And, yes, he had an answer. Of a sort. So this was not the time he would have to confess to Mrs Ahmed. Perhaps that time, after all, would never come.

He leant back and whispered.

'The compound at Shivram Patel's, it was most disgracefully neglected. And with the rain it had already become highly muddy. My trouser would have got extremely dirty there.'

He turned back to listen to R.K.

But R.K. seemed to have abandoned the question of the muddiness of the uniform. Which seemed odd. And what was it he was fishing for now?

'And was there anything more that you, plainly an exceptionally observant person, noticed about those garments?'

The dhobi looked at him for a moment or two, as if to be sure that his answer would be the one that had been required. Then he spoke.

'Oh yes, yes, sahib. Something more.'

'Good. And what was that?'

'The buttons of the jacket, sahib. They had been cut off with a scissor so that they also would not be beaten when I am washing. But there was one of them that was different, sahib.'

'One? Different?'

'Oh, yes, sahib. Number Two button down, it had been torn off from the jacket. Not at all cut. I was seeing the ends of the threads, sahib.'

'Torn off? You are certain about that?'

'Oh, yes, sahib. Many, many people are accusing me of cutting off buttons to steal, so I am always looking to see what has been done.'

'Good. Excellent. And this was, let us be sure of it, the second button down? The Number Two button down?'

'That was it, sahib.'

'Good. I see. Thank you.'

But, Ghote thought in bewilderment, what on earth use to them can that evidence be? I picked up that button. Yes, certainly it did come off when I lifted up Desai's body and the threads would look different from the places where Protima cut off the other buttons. But I picked up that one. I know I did.

So what can this be about? What?

17

It was not long before Ghote learnt what the significance of the missing button was, something that was to prove a blow to the defence Mrs Ahmed had so far established for him that was more damaging than he could have imagined. But first she was merely concerned with cross-examining the frightened Vasantrao Chavan. About the button she could ask him nothing, since neither she nor Ghote had any notion of its importance. But, armed with what he had told her about the foul, muddy state of Shivram Patel's compound, she was enabled by her questioning to put what the dhobi had said about the mud on the uniform in a much less damning light.

R. K. Sankar seemed even less discomposed than usual, however, by the way this part of his case had been made to look merely fanciful. He rose impassively to tell the Board what witness he next proposed to produce.

'Mr Presiding Officer, you may feel that it is too late in the day for a further witness to be heard, especially one who, you will find, will substantiate a major portion of the case it has been my duty to put before you.'

'Well, Mr Sankar,' S. M. Motabhoy gravely answered, 'I do feel certainly we should not attempt today to hear a witness of major importance. Who is it you wish to call?'

R.K. unexpectedly turned and directed his full gaze at Ghote, abruptly rigid on his hard chair.

'Mr Presiding Officer,' he said, 'the witness I should like next to put before you is one Piraji by name. He will testify to having seen the accused in company with the late A.D.I.G. Kelkar proceeding at night through the byways of Vigatpore with between them on a bicycle the body of a dead man.'

'Very well, Mr Sankar. Tomorrow.'

Ghote hardly heard S. M. Motabhoy. What R.K. had said boomed like a knell in his head.

He wanted not to believe it was possible. There could not have been a witness to that dreadful procession of his and Tiger's. The rain that night had been too absolutely blotting-out for it to have been possible. And yet, of course, it was possible. It had not been totally beyond anyone's powers to make their way beneath that sheeting, spearing downpour. He and Tiger had done it, after all. So someone else could have been out under it too.

But if there had been someone there to see them, someone whose evidence had been cunningly kept back by R.K. and Pimputkar till this moment, then this was the end of it all.

Yes, he thought, now I shall have to own up to everything. I shall have to tell them just what it was that I did. Nothing else for it. To tell them, and take the consequences. Finish of police work. Finish of service. Finish of everything.

The members of the Board, however, seemed to have taken R.K.'s dramatic announcement much in their stride. They had got to their feet and were putting on their uniform caps preparatory to going out. One or two of them were looking anxiously at the windows to see what the weather was doing. The rain, which had slackened to little more than a drizzle, was now coming down insistently once more. The window panes were awash and the tossing palms lining the Maidan no more than blurred shapes against the tumbled grey of the sky.

Ghote turned to Mrs Ahmed. But she, too, was simply bundling papers back into her big battered bag.

He remembered her calm attitude at the start of the Inquiry when R.K. had listed the events of the night in Vigatpore in such detail that he himself had momentarily panicked. Then she had said they should wait till the actual evidence had been produced and she had cross-examined the witnesses. No doubt she was treating R.K.'s announcement now in the same down-to-earth way.

But then she did not know that the new witness would be speaking no more than the truth. He must tell her.

'Madam,' he said, 'could we kindly have a few minutes of talk.'

To his surprise Mrs Ahmed looked up at him with an expression of plain annoyance.

'Inspector, I am sorry, but the Footpathwasi Kriti Samiti is taking out a procession against compulsory clearance of pavement dwellings during monsoon period. I have promised to join in presenting the petition, and already I am late.'

Ghote could not keep the hurt he felt off his face. Ready to pour out his confession, it had not occurred to him that Mrs Ahmed might not be ready to hear it. To hear it and to condemn him.

'Inspector,' she said hurriedly, 'I am really very sorry. But a promise is a promise. Look, tomorrow morning I will come one quarter of an hour early. Would that be enough time?'

'Yes, madam,' Ghote said. 'That will be enough of time. More than enough. Thank you.'

What I have to say, he thought, can be quickly said. Two or three sentences only of the truth, and it will be done.

He took his cap, tramped down and found his plastic cape and gumboots – S. M. Motabhoy, he saw, had no rain protection and was having to run in his uniform across the pavement to where his driver was waiting with his car – and went out to face the long scooter ride home through the piled up, impatient traffic and the swirling beating rain.

It took him even longer than usual to reach home, and even having to battle with the traffic and the rain did not prevent him thinking more and more despondently about the disaster which seemed to be about to topple down on him now like a huge poised rock. But, however grim the outcome would be, nothing altered his decision that all he could do was to end the lying and tell first Mrs Ahmed, then the whole Inquiry that he had indeed done what R.K.'s new witness was going to state that he had done.

So as soon as he had peeled off his plastic cape, almost as wet inside from condensation as it was outside from rain, and kicked off his gumboots he beckoned Protima into the kitchen. There, he hoped, Ved, sitting with his ear close to the radio on its shelf listening to the Bournvita Quiz, would not hear.

Then, with hardly a moment to pluck up his resolution, he told her that after all he was going to let the Inquiry hear the truth.

'No,' came the compacted monosyllable of her reply.

He thought for a moment that this was to be her only response. And, though the word had been spoken with explosive force, he felt it was an amount of opposition he could overcome.

But, of course, it was not all there was.

'Think, think,' Protima began to plead when words were restored to her. 'If you will not think of me, if you will not think of yourself, think of Ved only. How is he to become fully educated if after tomorrow you are without any income? You yourself said it: it would not be easy for a dismissed officer to find more employment. And then where are school fees, and college fees also to come from? Would you have Ved go to work? At the age that he is? Like a millworker's son? Would you do that to your child?'

'It may not come to so much,' he countered.

'But it would. You have said and said. Dismissal is what faces you.'

'It may not be so bad. The Show Cause notice might state only "Reduction in rank".'

'And you know that it will not.'

He hung his head. It was true, if now he were to admit after so many lies, so much evasion, that all along the truth had been just as the Inquiry charges had alleged, then it was only to be expected that S. M. Motabhoy would fix on the severest punishment within his powers. Dismissal. It would certainly be dismissal.

Protima put a hand on his arm. He smelt suddenly a faint whiff of raw onion from the meal she had been preparing. Cooking for him, as she had done ever since the first day of their marriage when, with such pride, she had made what his mother had told her was his favourite dish, sweet carrot halwa. He felt, a sweeping flood-tide, in that single gesture of hers all that the years of their marriage had brought to them in closeness, in affection, in physical togetherness, in love. He must not now, in these days of crisis, lose all that they had given each other. He must trust her. Trust her through and through.

'My husband, why must you do this now? What has happened that you have gone back on what you had promised?'

So, painfully, he told her in full detail how R.K. with behind him Inspector Pimputkar, that mongoose, had so carefully laid out his case to look at its very blackest at this point.

Protima was silent when he had finished. But at last she spoke, slowly and hesitantly.

'Husbandji, again I am begging. But for this only. Wait one day more, till you have heard-heard what this Piraji they are calling has said. It may not be as bad as they are promising. It may be the fellow thought only that he had seen you and Kelkar Sahib.'

Ghote heaved a long sigh.

'But there is the button,' he said. 'He will tell, I am certain,

167

that he saw that missing button. Why else was R.K. so keen to get that evidence from our dhobi?'

'But you will wait all the same? One day more only? Or two. It is Saturday tomorrow. Wait until Monday because the Inquiry will not be held on Sunday, will it?'

'Very well,' Ghote said, beaten down by all the weight of their shared past. 'I will leave it till Monday. But till then only.'

And at that moment Ved burst through the bead curtain behind them, face shining in simple uninhibited triumph.

'Dada. Dada. The Bournvita Quiz. I knew every answer.'

Ghote looked at his son with fierce pleasure, behind which there beat sickening fears for his future. Was he himself still going to imperil it all? He refused to think.

Chastened and still exhausted, next morning Ghote felt not a little embarrassment as he left early so as to meet Mrs Ahmed at the hour she had promised him to be there. Now, after all, he had nothing to say to her.

He arrived at the Old Secretariat even earlier than he needed, and stood waiting, going over in his mind the rather feeble excuses he had concocted.

The minutes passed.

He looked at his watch. Mrs Ahmed was already five minutes later than the hour she had given him.

More time went by. Had she perhaps realised that what R.K.'s witness was going to say must be true? And had she simply abandoned him? And rightly so.

But, when there were only two or three minutes before the Inquiry was due to resume she appeared, running and looking uncharacteristically ruffled beneath her rain-streaming umbrella.

'Inspector, I am sorry to be late. A waterlogging. Some boys, I suspect, had blocked a drain. But when my husband's car reached they were not there to push us through.'

'Nothing to worry, nothing to worry,' Ghote assured her, relieved to an extraordinary extent.

Together they hurried up the stairs, along the photo-graph-lined corridor and entered the big room just as S. M. Motabhoy was looking round to see if everybody was ready to begin.

'Mr Sankar,' he said, when he had waited for Mrs Ahmed to dump some papers from her heavy bag on her desk. 'You had a new witness for us.'

'Yes, Mr Presiding Officer. I call one Piraji, from Vigatpore.'

There was some delay, but not a long one, before this mysterious person who had, according to R.K., actually seen the two of them with the body on the bicycle was led in.

Ghote looked at him with fierce anxiety. What could he make of this man who had been so cunningly kept in reserve by R.K. and Pimputkar finally to undo him? The man who, for whatever reason, had been out on that first night of the monsoon and who when the rain had begun to ease off had seen them in the dim orangey moonlight from the shadows. Only, why was he in the shadows? This man who had seen the place where on his own uniform a button was missing?

Plainly the fellow was poor. He was wearing only a checked red lungi wrapped round his waist and a thin shirt with an unmended rip just below its single pocket. On his head he had a white headcloth – only it was, rather, a dirty grey.

So not exactly a respectable witness. But if he were to speak up and tell his truth with conviction it would be enough. It would discount the effect of a face pitted with smallpox scars and the twist in his long nose.

'You are one by name Piraji?'

R.K.'s questions had begun, the questions that were in all likelihood to lead to the final truth of that night in Vigatpore.

'I am Piraji, maharaj.'

'Piraji, do you remember a certain night, the first of the monsoon, in Vigatpore last year?'

'Very well I am remembering, maharaj.'

'That night you were in a certain backlane near the edge of the town, not far from the lake there?'

'I was, maharaj.'

The fellow, despite his villainous face, was speaking up well. S. M. Motabhoy would not be influenced by a twisted nose and smallpox marks. He would accept the fellow's evidence as true.

As it was. As it was.

'At about what hour was this? Can you say?'

'I cannot say very well, maharaj. But from the time I was leaving my home, which is five miles from Vigatpore, it must have been after midnight.'

'After midnight? You are sure of that?'

'Ji, maharaj.'

'It could not have been an hour earlier?'

'Nai, nai, maharaj. Past-past midnight.'

Still firm in everything he was saying. No trying to make out he could tell the time to the minute. No talk of non-existent clocks. Just this plain statement that he had left his house some five miles out of Vigatpore at a time that would have brought him to that backlane at much the hour he and Tiger had actually been there.

But what on earth was the fellow doing at that hour at such a spot? Why had he left home at –

The answer came into Ghote's mind with the certainty of a line being drawn under a simple sum of addition and the answer set down.

He turned urgently to Mrs Ahmed.

'A history-sheeter,' he whispered. 'Nothing but a history-sheeter.'

'Yes,' she whispered back after she had heard him out. 'Yes, I was beginning to wonder. But are you sure?'

'The more I am thinking, the more certain I am.'

Behind Ghote as he whispered, R.K.'s steady questioning continued punctuated by his witness's easy answers and that reiterated, obsequious 'maharaj', 'maharaj'.

'And there was a button missing from his uniform?'

'Ji, maharaj.'

'Which button? Can you say?'

'Ji, maharaj. Second button down.'

'And that man, that police officer in uniform with one button, the second one down, missing, pulling along that bicycle with on it a man who appeared certainly to be dead, can you see him here in this room now?'

'Ji, maharaj. He is there.'

And the pock-marked man's outstretched arm and extended forefinger pointed directly at Ghote sitting, back stiffly upright, on his hard chair.

'Thank you, Piraji. That is all. That is enough.'

Mrs Ahmed rose to her feet then, quite slowly, adjusting the drab green sari under the white barrister's bands round her neck.

'Piraji, from what community do you come?'

Ghote, watching not the witness but R.K., lolling behind his table with its impressive piles of papers, thought he detected on that never-angered face one tiny spasm of rage.

'I am of the Mahadev Koli community.'

'And most members of that community live near Vigatpore?'

'Yes. Near.'

Mrs Ahmed drew herself up a little.

'The Mahadev Koli community,' she said blandly. 'And you know, doubtless, that in Kennedy's authoritative book on the criminal tribes of India your community is described as one whose members leave their lair only to commit robberies and dacoities, and that though in recent times –'

R.K. was on his feet and almost shouting.

'Mr Presiding Officer, this is disgraceful. The witness cannot be expected to answer such a question. What does he know of Kennedy's book or any other?'

S. M. Motabhoy up at his long table gave a hint of a smile.

'Yes, Mr Sankar,' he said. 'The question was expecting

rather more of your witness than he was likely to be able to provide. But then, since you omitted to ask him where he came from, Mrs Ahmed was perhaps justified in drawing the Board's attention to his antecedents in the way she chose.'

R.K. sank back on to his chair.

'Mrs Ahmed,' S. M. Motabhoy continued, 'I accept that the witness is in fact of such dubious reputation, a member of a caste of professional robbers, that we cannot in justice hear him. No doubt he was in Vigatpore that night for the purposes of his profession and he is lucky to find himself sent back home at public expense with no further questions asked.'

Ghote felt as if, tossed hither and thither on some great river in full flood, miraculously a log or a raft or some solid object had come up from beneath him and lifted him to safety.

S. M. Motabhoy watched the unfortunate Piraji being hustled from the room. Then he gave his resounding cough.

'And now,' he said, 'though the day is not far advanced I am going to adjourn until Monday morning. I have an engagement I must attend, and I had hoped the Inquiry would have concluded its business before this. However, we have not done so.'

He turned again to R.K.

'And on Monday,' he said, 'I think we had better hear from Inspector Pimputkar once more. He seems to have been somewhat unfortunate, to say the least, in the witnesses he has found.'

Ghote was hardly aware after this of the Inquiry breaking up. Mrs Ahmed did ask him what it was he had wanted to say to her first thing, and he managed to stammer out that it no longer mattered. She seemed to assume it had been something to do with the evidence Piraji had been going to give and, stuffing her papers into her bag, she left in her accustomed hurry.

Ghote left then in his turn.

But as he sat astride his scooter before attempting to kick start it, he pondered over the escape he had had.

It had been miraculous, yes. But it had also been his own doing. If he had not realised that Pimputkar had got hold of a witness the Board were bound to consider tainted and if he had not pointed out to Mrs Ahmed what community the fellow was likely to be from, even recalling from police college that authoritative book, by now all would have been lost. Of course, Pimputkar must have hit on the notion that if anyone was about in Vigatpore on such a night it might be a thief, and he had probably consulted Inspector Khan's ill-kept Bad Character Roll and had at last tracked down Piraji. It was clever of him, damned clever. But he had been outwitted.

With a flare-up of sheer pride, he kicked his machine into life and set off. Only to find that, underneath, he had come to a resolve in exactly the contrary sense.

He was not going to go on hoping that with luck and occasional cleverness he could continue to outsmart Pimputkar. Because however cunning the fellow was, however unscrupulous, the fact remained that he was trying to prove a case that was true. And even his tainted witness, the dacoit, the professional thief, had been speaking no less than the truth.

On that night in Vigatpore he himself had done just what Pimputkar had guessed that he had.

No, he had promised Protima that he would say nothing until Monday. But on Monday he would stand up before the Inquiry and tell the whole truth at last. No more wriggling. No more evading. He had done what he had done, and he would own up to it.

18

Ghote said nothing of his new determination when he reached home. He had made up his mind and would not change it, however sudden his decision had been. And he did not at all welcome the infuriated opposition he would have to face if he were to tell Protima. He did bring himself, with reluctance, to give her at least an account of what had happened at the Inquiry, and he endured in silence her evident satisfaction at having, as she thought, prevented him from making an unnecessary confession.

The effort left him nervy and irritable. The sharp-smelling dampness everywhere, which in other years he had happily ignored, seemed to enter into his very body. He sneezed and shook himself.

'You are catching cold,' Protima said. 'You must change your shirt. You should have done it when you were first coming back.'

'No, no. I am quite all right.'

'No, you must. If you are taking a fever just only now it would be very bad. Remember, the Inquiry goes on on Monday also.'

'I know when the Inquiry is.'

'But if you have to face questioning by that R. K. Sankar when your head is full of cold only . . .'

'It will not be full of cold,' he snarled.

Why, why did she have to remind him of the ordeal which sooner or later he would have to face again? R.K.'s full-scale questioning, cold in the head or no cold, would be quite bad enough.

But then a thought bloomed secretly in his head. He was not going to have to face that questioning. As soon as the Inquiry reopened he would stand up and say he had a statement to make. Then he would tell them, without any lies, without dodging anything, just what had happened that night. And the Inquiry would come to an end.

R.K.'s icy task would be over. Inspector Pimputkar's investigation could be left on the file. All that would remain would be for S. M. Motabhoy to decide what punishment he should award and enter it on the Show Cause notice. And that would be that.

What would happen afterwards would happen. If it was 'Dismissal', as was almost certain, he would not think of contesting it. He would surrender uniform, belt, warrant card, everything. And then he would do what he could to scrape some sort of a living somehow.

It would be the end of all his hopes. But, in truth, their end had come at the moment when he had put himself at Tiger's disposal. There could be no going back from that. Any idea that there had been was illusion only.

The thought of how utterly complete his ruin would be wiped away with paradoxical comfort all the irritation he had been feeling.

'Well, if you are insisting,' he said to Protima, 'I will put on another shirt. If it is not damp also.'

Protima ignored this last little jibe – it had been in any case half-hearted – and found him a shirt which she had managed to keep dry. He put it on, and succeeded in rejecting without

175

rancour her immediate next suggestion, that he should munch a raw onion.

Next morning the rain had blessedly come to a temporary halt. Looking out, Ghote saw that the sun had even begun to shine again. Wet surfaces everywhere, black tarmac, huge puddles, grey pavements, were glinting and gleaming. His hard-won subdued cheerfulness of the day before bounded up into a state of positive well-being. The future might be grim – he did not let himself think precisely about it – but at least it was settled. Next day, in one short statement to the officers of the Inquiry he would lift the torturing weight from his shoulders once and for all.

'I think I will go and eat a whiff of air,' he said to Protima. 'It is nice to see the sun for a little.'

'No,' she said unexpectedly.

'No?'

She stood for a moment, a small frown of thought on her forehead.

'No. Please, the drainages at the back have become blocked. There is very nasty smell. Can you take some Expel and clear them? You must put four to five tablespoons at the mouth of each and then pour on boiling water.'

Ghote felt a little put out. He did not usually object to such domestic tasks. A certain amount of feminine incapability was flattering. But the sight of the sun, often dreaded but today enlivening, had made him keen to take his stroll and to have that impulse unexpectedly checked was annoying.

'But cannot Ved do such a simple task?' he asked. 'The boy is always playing and playing. It is time he learnt that there are duties also.'

'Playing and playing? He is not at all playing always. Look how well he studies. Look how good he is in squeezing out the towels at the windows.'

'Well, he can do this also.'

'No. No, I am not wanting you to go out this morning.'

'Ah, that is it, is it? But why are you wishing me to be pegged down in the house only?'

Protima looked abruptly sullen.

'And why should I not?' she asked. 'You are so much away. Why should I not be wanting you for once to be here?'

'But I have been here and here ever since I have been under suspension itself. And you were complaining against me then.'

'Well, now I am not complain –'

A loud hooting from a car outside brought her to a halt. Surprisingly, she hurried across and looked out.

'Oh,' she said. 'Look who has come.'

What on earth . . . Ghote thought.

He went over to the window in his turn.

And then he understood.

Drawn up immediately outside was a foreign-made car, one of the few in Bombay. Though it was not new, it gave off an evident air of ostentation, considerably enhanced by the large, tough-looking driver in the front bursting out of a white uniform with a cap with a shiny black peak.

Ghote turned to Protima.

'It is Ram Bhaskar,' he said. 'You have asked him to come. That is why you were not wanting me to go out. That was why also you were asking me to wait before I was telling the truth to the Inquiry.'

'What if it is Bhaskar Sahib?' Protima answered. 'He is your oldest friend, isn't it?'

Ghote stood speechless and at a loss.

Yes, Ram Bhaskar was his oldest friend. The two of them had been friends, sometimes friendly enemies, right from the days when he had been the schoolmaster's son and Ram the son of the temple pujari, a father he had perhaps driven into bitterness because of the tremendous, uninhibited youthful rages that had got him into every sort of trouble – besides making him the unanimous choice to take the part of the fierce demon Ravana in the annual Ramayana play.

He and Ram had had many a ding-dong, argument, many a fight. One in particular Ghote recalled. It had almost brought an end to the friendship, though what it had started over neither of them afterwards had been able to remember. But he could see them both now, standing under the jackfruit tree at the edge of the village pond. Each had succeeded during the struggle in breaking the other's brahmin's thread, a serious enough crime, and each was, dark with anger, standing glaring at the other. Which of them had pronounced the unsayable words first? *I put a brahmin's curse upon you*. The curse, they had fervently believed then, that could not be taken back.

And, Ghote was sure, though neither of them when the wild quarrel had mysteriously resolved itself had ever referred to those shouted words again, neither had ever quite forgotten them.

Was Ram Bhaskar's puff of a curse coming true for himself now? Certainly he had never been in a worse trouble. And his own once believed-in curse? Well, despite the foreign car and the driver in uniform, Ram's career – he had gone into business, profit-mad as any Marwari – had not been spotless. As the years had gone by, he himself had taken good care not to know too much about it. Section 420 of the Indian Penal Code, cheating, no doubt applied. Indeed, Ram seemed to be a fine example of what people called an 'eight-forty', a double-dyed cheat. And yet the friendship had maintained itself, however long the gaps between seeing each other, however far apart their lives had grown. Really it was ridiculously like a typical Hindi film, two brothers separated in youth one to become the Hero, the other the Villain.

And Protima had known, much though she disapproved of this notorious figure from his past, just how strong the friendship still was. She knew that Ram was perhaps the one person of his own age who could influence him. So, of course, she had wrung out of him that promise of delay and had summoned the demon to her aid.

Out in the road, Ghote saw Ram step from his car, cigarette in mouth, stocky, walking almost with a wrestler's gait up on the balls of his feet. There was a faint smile on his lips though there was no one there to smile at. He was wearing a light tan suit in what, even at a distance, was plainly raw silk.

Yes, Ram had done well for himself. Moving from one business to another just before the bad times or the Customs Investigators came. Was he still the owner of that fire-crackers factory? Perhaps he had got rid of it now.

There came a loud cheerful knocking at the door.

'Well,' Protima said, 'are you going to let him in? He is your friend from boyhood.'

With a tumble of feelings, Ghote drew back the door bolt and admitted Ram. With great pattings of each other's backs they embraced. Protima, hovering discreetly, offered tea or a cold drink.

'Hard stuff,' Ram said breezily. 'You know I am always drinking hard stuff.'

'At the start of the morning?' Ghote answered, a grin creakily forcing its way on to his face.

'Oh, well, I cannot be expecting such a good-good police-walla to have a whisky bottle ready. Tea it will have to be.'

Protima went to the kitchen.

Ram threw himself down in the one comfortable chair and thrust out his legs.

'So, what is this I am hearing?' he said. 'Ganesh Ghote suspended. Up before big-big Inquiry. And wanting to say *I am guilty-guilty, forgive, forgive?*'

'So Protima was telling you everything?'

'Of course, of course. Sensible woman you got yourself there, Ganeshji. Always said. Beautiful also.'

'Well, if you have come to persuade,' Ghote answered,

'you can drink your tea and get back into that great big car you have.'

'And you are still riding scooter?'

'Yes. Yes, I am. But soon I will have to sell.'

'Because they are going to neck you out of the police, bhai?'

'Yes.'

'Well, it might be the best thing, you know. You could get down to some business-business then and make some money-money.'

Ghote's old friend gave him a quick shrewd glance.

'But, no,' he laughed. 'I know that is not what you were wanting ever to do in life. Damn fool you, but that's the way you are. Wanting and wanting always only to be a policewalla.'

He sat up suddenly in the comfortable chair.

'You remember that missionary fellow used to come to the village?' he said. 'You wanted to keep King-Emperor's peace even then, when we were all throwing mud and stones at the fellow. How years fly off. But you remember that?'

Ghote did, and smiled. It had been when they were both no more than nine or ten. For some reason a European missionary had taken to coming to the village, a solemn, pale-faced fellow lurking under a large sola topee with a stiff, shiny white round collar ringing his scrawny neck. He had been accompanied by varying groups of converts armed with a harmonium and one or two other musical instruments. Sometimes there had been a trumpet which had produced only occasional supporting notes, either much too loud or feebly squeaky. After they had gathered a crowd by singing a hymn or two, the missionary would speak in terrible banging Marathi. On the first occasion it had even taken his listeners some while to make out he was talking in their language at all. But then, when it had penetrated that he was actually urging them to throw the temple idol into the village pond and 'come to Jesus meek and mild', tempers had flared.

And it had been Ram, boy that he was, who had been fiercest among them all, shouting and black with rage, perhaps in defence of the pujari, his father, with whom he did nothing but quarrel. And mud had flown, and, yes, a stone or two. Rapid retreat of converts. But brave stand-by missionary. Till the very last gasp of his sermon 'Remember then these words of the Bible. *Yea, I do well to be angry even unto death.*' As if any one of them had read the Christian's Bible to remember anything from it, as if more than two or three of them could even understand the English the fellow had dropped into for his quotation.

Though, oddly, he himself had remembered the words through all the years. From time to time they floated into his mind – at the most unlikely moments.

Protima came in with the tea.

'Well, Bhaskar Sahib,' she said when they had drunk a little, 'have you spoken to this husband of mine?'

'He has,' Ghote answered. 'And no good has it done him.'

Ram laughed.

'Nai, nai, bhai. I am not even beginning.'

Still feeling his resentment like an iron rod down his back, Ghote refused to let Ram's cheerfulness move him.

'You had better not begin itself,' he said. 'Recall old days if you like. But do not interfere with what I myself am doing today.'

'You are afraid I will lose my temper and give you a beating like the day we quarrelled by the jack-fruit tree?' Ram asked, eyes sparkling.

'If beating was given, I was the one giving.'

'But who got his thread broken?'

Ram grinned broadly.

'If you really remember that,' Ghote said, 'you would know that both our threads were broken. But you were the most angry.'

Ram wagged his head.

'Yes, I am sure I was. In those days I was angry at

everything. But now, you know, I never lose my temper. Not once.'

'No, that I am not believing,' Ghote shot out.

'But it is true-true.'

Ram winked then.

'I am not knowing whether it is plenty of booze or plenty of charas, Inspectorji,' he added. 'But I promise you, never now do I get at all angry.'

'But your business?' Ghote asked despite himself, so amazed was he by Ram's claim, which nevertheless, knowing him through and through as he did, he found he fully believed. 'How do you make a success of your business without shouting and cursing?'

Ram laughed.

'Business is fine,' he said. 'You were seeing the car I have now? Things go from good to better, and not only because people are bursting more and more of fire-crackers. No, by using plenty-plenty child labour, defying every day Minimum Wages Act, and by making many-many prohibited types, ukhali daru exceeding ten centimetres in length and tadtady throw-downs, I do nicely-nicely. And all without one word of cursing.'

Ghote – he had the canework stool – sat in silence for a moment or two, still absorbing the fact of the transformation in his boyhood friend. Then he answered dully.

'Well, I am not going to report you and your tadtady throw-downs, even if what you are saying is not just only your joking. In one day's time I shall no longer be the little police officer who wanted always to keep order when the missionary walla came to the village.'

'Oh, but you will be,' Ram said. 'You cannot help. And you can report-report as much as you like. Two-three bribes will take care of all.'

'No,' Ghote shot back in sudden fury. 'You need not think that each and every time a bribe will get you out of trouble. Not every officer in the police is corrupt.'

Ram leant back in his comfortable chair and roared with laughter.

'You see, little policewalla, you are a police officer still. I said it: you cannot shake yourself out of that, however hard you are trying. Not if you shake and shake till Shiva destroys the world.'

Ghote felt caught out. Caught out as he had often been by this best friend in his boyhood. By some riddle, or some joke, or some tongue-twister. But caught out now more deeply. By the truth. Ram had cleverly ripped to pieces that whole edifice of belief he had constructed that he could after all accept no longer being a police officer. It was as if, as he had seen once, a blast of monsoon wind had seized an old sari used as a curtain by a wretched family living in a huge waterpipe waiting to be dug in and had shredded it to rags to reveal all inside.

Yes, oh yes, he still wanted in his heart's core to do the job that he had done all his life.

And – a yet worse thought grew up in his mind – there was the other thing Ram had said, the fact he had yet to tackle in his mind.

That Ram never now lost his temper. That he ran his business with success without resorting to anger, without shouting, without the least bite of rage.

It was extraordinary. Ram, Ram whose whole being on the surface had always consisted of that exploding temper, now to be, not placid, but free of those instant descents, or ascents, into wild, uncontrolled rage. If Ram had been, in their old village days, always the chosen Ravana, the fierce demon, when the Ramayana plays had been enacted, then had a supernatural being somehow changed sides? Had the demon god become a good god?

Could such a change happen in human nature?

Yes. Yes, it could. It had. Though Ram could and would lie and lie, in business, in trouble, to bring off a joke or a jape, he himself had always known when such a lie was being given out. He knew Ram as well as he knew himself. He had always done. So, yes, it seemed that it was possible for someone, who appeared to be ruled in all he did by the sudden fire-cracker rages he was heir to, to overcome that entrenched weakness. To become a new man.

Or, not quite that. More, he thought, knowing Ram as he had done from very earliest days, more to shed an unnecessary outer casing and to fall back to the true shape underneath. Yes, that was a possible thing.

But –

But – the sudden thought came to him – but that had not been Tiger Kelkar's way. The way he himself had believed he must go. The way he had come to think was the only right way for a good police officer, one who existed not to fill his own pockets but to put right the wrongs in his world.

He realised now, sitting on his stool in emptied silence opposite a cheerfully grinning Ram, that in fact he had never in the depths of his being truly believed in the way of anger, however much he had told himself that Tiger was the example to follow, however much he had done to prove that to himself.

Had he not all along had a counter-example there to see, little though he had brought it to mind? But he had had the memory of old Nadkarni there, as alive as that of Tiger until Tiger had come into his life in vigorous person once more. And had he ever in all the time he had worked under and even alongside that patient old spider seen him in rage? Never by a hair's breadth. And yet he had admired him. And still did admire him, puny and aged though he had now become. Because he had not been puny in the days when he had been in his seat. With him you would never think, as he had thought so often with poor Shinde in Vigatpore, of 'Lords without anger or honour, who dare not carry their swords.' Nadkarni, ever quiet, ever calm, had carried his sword always.

So, if Tiger's way was not the only way, or even the better way for him himself, what had become of all that had begun on that dreadful night in Vigatpore?

19

In the state of emptiness in which Ghote found himself with his realisation that attachment to Tiger Kelkar was not the only pattern he could follow, it had needed none of Ram Bhaskar's persuasion to make him decide after all not to break his promise to conceal the truth from the Inquiry. Ram had been forceful about 'taking a practical view'. He had even offered to bribe S. M. Motabhoy to make some legal error, perhaps in the Show Cause notice he might eventually have to fill out. But it had all been unnecessary.

'Bribing that man is something even you could not be doing,' Ghote had concluded. 'But in any case if I stick to my story, now that they have discounted that criminal Piraji, there cannot be any evidence strong enough for it to go against me.'

'And you will not be foolish-foolish and spill each and every bean yourself?' Ram had asked.

'No, no. You were right. What I want is to stay as a police officer. It is what I can do, and I will tell this one lie to my level best so that I may go on doing it.'

But things did not turn out to be quite as simple as he had then thought.

On Monday the rain, which had resumed its downpour on

Sunday afternoon and had continued unabated all night, abruptly eased off just as he was setting out, in good time, for the Inquiry. In consequence he arrived more than twenty minutes before proceedings were due to begin. And so did Mrs Ahmed. Aware of her behind him as he sat waiting in the big room, a series of new thoughts assailed him.

Why was he still deceiving this fighter for truth, this enemy of hypocrisies? He was taking up her time purely for his own selfish reasons. He was letting her support his lie when she could be working for the pavement dwellers whose huts were in danger of being bulldozed in full monsoon or the stairways refugees from the slum at Worli. Or, even, there was the person who had put together that long, indignant purple-typed protest.

No, was he not putting himself and his problems altogether too much to the fore? His mind full of nothing but whether he ought to lie so as to go on living the life he felt was the only one for him, he had forgotten even the man whose life ending had been the start of the whole business, poor stupid Sergeant Desai. He had forgotten him, as he had altogether forgotten Desai's bhabhi, the girl full of guts whose husband had had his brother unjustly taken from him. And he had admired the bhabhi. He had felt himself on her side when at Headquarters she had stood up to the A.C.P. in his own office.

But now, full of his own troubles, all other thoughts had been driven out. Mrs Ahmed, had he really thought again about the slumdwellers she had taken him to see? Those men in the stinking lock-up? Those families in their wretched rain-dripping, flooded huts?

They had their troubles, worse than his. They had their lives somehow to live. As had Mrs Ahmed. And all for his own concerns he was putting her out of his mind, and, worse, taking up her time that could be being used, hard worker that she was, to good ends.

For some five minutes more he sat and squirmed while

these thoughts ran through his head. Then he got up and leant over the desk behind him.

'Mrs Ahmed, madam,' he said, 'there is something I am wishing to tell.'

Mrs Ahmed looked up from a legal document she had been perusing – a writ in yet another case she had taken up? – and gave him a friendly glance.

'Well, what is it I can do for you?'

For a moment Ghote was silent, suddenly not knowing how he was to say what he was now fully determined to come out with, At last he made an effort.

'Madam, I regret that I have all along been deceiving.'

'Deceiving, Inspector?'

A quick frown had appeared on her broad forehead.

Ghote swallowed.

'Yes, deceiving. The truth of the matter is that each thing that they have been saying about me is one hundred percent correct. Yes, it was not until 3 a.m. that I was returning to Shivram Patel's house. Yes, I was there in that office when A.D.I.G. Kelkar threw the inkpot at Sergeant Desai. It was even I myself who suggested to him he should not submit to arrest at my hands and, because Desai had very much boasted of his swimming powers and taken up bets thereon, that he should put his body into Lake Helena. And that we were doing together. Yes, even that fellow Piraji, member of a criminal tribe though he is, was telling the truth when I was not.'

Mrs Ahmed sat in silence once his long, tumbling explanation was over.

'Madam, please,' Ghote said at last, 'what are you going to do?'

'Inspector, I have the feeling that you are not intending to tell all this to the Inquiry. Am I right?'

'Yes, madam.'

'Why, Inspector?'

Ghote paused a moment before replying.

'Well, it is this,' he said. 'Except and bar this one only thing, I have been a good police officer always. A damn good police officer, though I am saying. So I am wishing, if it is in any way possible, to go on being a police officer.'

Mrs Ahmed was silent again for a little.

'I suppose it might be possible,' she said. 'I had up till now believed it was going in our favour. In your favour.'

'In mine only?'

'Yes,' Mrs Ahmed said. 'In yours alone. Let me tell you this, Inspector. I will no more come to your assistance. I will not back you up if you are intending to go on with your lie. But one thing I will do, not altogether willingly but because I believe you are a good police officer, one of not so many. I will continue to sit here. You must at least appear to be represented, and it is too late now for you to find a substitute.'

'Yes, madam,' Ghote said, not having thought of this.

'So today when R. K. Sankar brings his case to its end by calling Inspector Pimputkar I will not, as I had intended, cross-examine to show there is a degree of animus against you. Nor will I call you yourself in my turn. You will have some chance to put your case when you make your Defendant's Statement. You must do with that what you can.'

'Yes. I understand. It is most good for you.'

He went back and sat down.

Through his mind there passed what he imagined the morning's proceedings would now be like. R.K. would take Pimputkar through his evidence uninterrupted by any sharp questions. Every insinuation would be allowed to tell to its fullest. R.K. after a little would look with barely concealed wonder over at Mrs Ahmed sitting unmoved at his every daring bending of the strict truth. Then at last he would tell S. M. Motabhoy that he rested his case. And S. M. Motabhoy, with all his rounded courtesy, would ask Mrs Ahmed to call her witnesses, and she would simply say that she did not intend to call any. S. M. Motabhoy, surely, would then ask, in astonishment, whether she did not even mean to call the accused and again she would say that she did not.

So they would come to his own Defendant's Statement when he would simply repeat his denial that he had known anything about Tiger's disposing of Desai's body. And then . . . Then there would come the moment when the Board's decision was made known.

Would it be in his favour? Or with such evidence as had been put before them going unchallenged, especially what Pimputkar would now find to say, would they after all find against him?

It was hard to tell. But if it did go against him then S. M. Motabhoy would simply write down on the Show Cause notice – he had glimpsed it already there on the table, waiting – what punishment he proposed and sign and date it. But what would the punishment be? Dismissal, almost certainly. Perhaps, if S. M. Motabhoy was markedly lenient, only compulsory retirement. But that would be just as bad. And it would be the very least a fair man like S. M. Motabhoy could impose on an officer who had persisted in concealing a major crime.

As he had. As he had.

When the Inquiry resumed it seemed to go, uncannily, almost exactly as he had foreseen. It all echoed unpleasantly the very first day of the proceedings when R.K. had, mysteriously as it had then seemed, recounted all but exactly what he and Tiger had done the night they had disposed of poor Desai's lumbering body.

Pimputkar was called and, taut-faced, burning with inner zeal, was taken through his evidence. He said nothing that was particularly new, but, skilfully guided by R.K. he contrived to present the findings of his investigation at their most damning. And, as at each malicious twist Mrs Ahmed failed to rise in challenge, R.K. did glance across at her in increasing amazement. Then when at last he announced that he rested his case and S. M. Motabhoy asked Mrs Ahmed to present hers – it was like a dream, a nightmare, coming true by daylight – she said simply that she did not intend to call any witnesses.

Yet, nightmare though it was, Ghote found that he was experiencing a tiny glim of content. His troubles had been caused by a decision that he felt had been right. And now he had freed Mrs Ahmed from the burden of innocently backing the lie he was telling in support of that decision. If that was putting him to torture now, well, so be it.

'You are not calling even Inspector Ghote?' S. M. Motabhoy asked, his eyebrows rising.

'No, Mr Presiding Officer.'

S. M. Motabhoy sat pondering for several long moments. Then, looking directly at Ghote, he spoke.

'I said at the outset of this Inquiry that our purpose was to elicit the truth and that, to that end, I did not consider we should necessarily be bound by the conventions and procedures of a court of law. It is my feeling that such a policy has been of benefit to us already, more than once. So, in the circumstances, I propose that we should again establish our own convention and that Mr Sankar should put to you, Inspector, such questions as he deems appropriate.'

Ghote felt sick.

To have to come up after all against R.K. once more, and unprotected now by an advocate of his own. Would he be able to hold out? He had survived that first unexpected short encounter when he had been questioned about whether he had a guru-chela relationship with Tiger. But now his whole defence, his whole lie, would fall under examination, and officers every bit as experienced as himself had told him how they had been made to feel like muddled erring schoolboys under the whiplash of R.K.'s tongue. And they had been giving evidence that was, for the most part, the simple truth.

R.K. began, quietly, by going back to the early part of that night more than a year before. Repeatedly consulting the papers on the table in front of him, he asked about each of the men in the police station who had been sent off duty at that time. Under this almost hypnotic questioning, Ghote found he was able to remember just what he had said and done in even greater detail than when he had listened to the men themselves saying, from this same witness table, what they had recalled of his orders. As R.K. asked each question he answered it truthfully and exactly. None gave him any trouble. After all, he had done just what he was telling R.K. he had done and there was nothing to hide about any of it.

'So, Inspector, by approximately the hour of 11 p.m. all the personnel in the station had been sent to their quarters?'

'Yes, sir. With the exception of the night sentry, who was outside, and of course myself.'

'Good. But, Inspector, are you not omitting one name?'

'A.D.I.G. Kelkar, sir? But I was not considering him as one of the station personnel.'

'I should hope not, Inspector. I should hope not.'

R.K. fell silent. Ghote waited for the next question.

'Well, Inspector?'

'Sir?'

'Have you not omitted one name? I wonder what the significance of that may be.'

'I am sorry, sir, I am not understanding.'

'No, Inspector? Is this perhaps because we have come to an area about which you would prefer to tell us nothing?'

'Sir?'

Ghote felt himself now suddenly all at sea. Dangerously at sea.

'Inspector, where was Sergeant Desai at this time?'

'I – I – Sergeant Desai is the whole subject of this Inquiry. I did not – It did not occur to me that you could be meaning him.'

'Indeed? But I have asked, Inspector, whether Sergeant Desai was present in the station at that time. Will you kindly bring yourself to answer?'

'Yes, sir. Yes, Sergeant Desai was present, though I myself was not aware of it.'

'I see. But you were aware later of Mr Kelkar throwing the inkpot at him?'

Ghote had to check back the affirmative almost on his lips. The abruptness with which they had entered the territory of pure fiction had almost caught him out.

'No, sir, no,' he managed to reply without, he hoped, his hesitation being too noticeable. 'I had left in my turn before Desai went in to take Mr Kelkar the F.I.R. he was requiring.'

'Ah. So Sergeant Desai went into Inspector Khan's office where A.D.I.G. Kelkar was at work, did he? And you knew this, although you had left the building? You were perhaps somewhere in that room, a disembodied spirit?'

'No, sir, no. No, I was saying, I had left the station before that took place.'

'And yet you knew all about it? Had every detail at your command?'

Ghote drew in a long breath.

'I did not have at my command every detail,' he said. 'I naturally knew Desai took in an F.I.R. and had an inkpot thrown at him. Mr Motabhoy was reading out A.D.I.G. Kelkar's account, here in this room itself.'

'Very well.'

R.K., while by no means looking discomposed, had spoken somewhat abruptly.

Ghote began to feel with this one small triumph that the whole examination, much more of it though there must be, might not be quite as bad as he had feared. If he could only keep his head, keep calm, he could survive without that truth coming to light.

But R. K. showed no other sign of feeling he had failed.

'Let us pass right on to another point,' he said. 'A matter about which we have already heard some evidence. Shri Shivram Patel's house. Tell me, your account of arriving there before midnight was sheer invention, was it not?'

'No. No, no, no.'

He realised then that, put out a little by the quick switch to a whole different part of his deception, he had shouted his answer. Had that shown he was lying? Perhaps it had.

'Methinks,' said R.K. in an audible aside, 'the gentleman doth protest too much.'

Ghote wondered what on earth he was talking about. What was this 'methinks'?

'How much before midnight?'

The snapped question caught him on the hop.

'I – I am sorry I was not hearing,' he said, conscious of how much the words might tell against him.

'Daydreaming, Inspector? Allowing full play to that vivid imagination which enabled you to see events in Inspector Khan's office, when, so you tell us, you had already left the building?'

Ghote felt, for more moments than he could have wished, baffled. What was he expected to answer? With an effort he pulled himself together.

'Your question is not entirely clear to me, sir,' he said. 'Would you kindly repeat same?'

R.K. gave a great theatrical sigh.

'Perhaps we had better let it pass. Perhaps instead you could manage to tell us how it was that you came to know the time so accurately when on a dark and cloudy night you stood at the door of Shri Patel's house and informed his servant so distinctly that it was not yet midnight?'

Ghote's mind raced, but came up with an instant answer.

'I had looked at the time in the station before my departure. And I was very well knowing how long it took to foot it from there to my quarter.'

'In the dark, inspector? In the heavy rain?'

'At that time the rain was not –'

He stopped himself. Good God, what had the rain been doing, not at 3 a.m., but just before midnight? It had been pouring hard, of course, not barely drizzling as it had been later.

He swallowed.

'Yes, Inspector? The rain was not what?'

'It was not – not my chief concern. I was keen only to get to bed after a long day.'

R.K. paused for a moment at that.

'Very well,' he resumed, 'now tell us about the boat, Inspector. Did you find it or did Mr Kelkar?'

But in the aftermath of his little victory over the rain Ghote was too alert to be caught by this.

'Boat, sir?' he said. 'I am not understanding you.'

'The boat you used to convey Sergeant Desai's body to the middle of Lake Helena, Inspector.'

'But I was not at all doing that.'

But had he been too heated even in that denial? If he had truly tramped back to Shivram Patel's house before even Desai had gone in to Tiger, would he not have answered the question with more calm? Heated anger was surely a sign of a bad conscience.

He resolved from that moment to keep a stricter guard on himself.

And he succeeded. On occasions that R.K. paused to consult the notes on the table in front of him before starting on some new line of questioning he actually had a moment once or twice to feel a little proud of the calm he was managing to show despite the increasingly sarcastic tone of the examination.

'And that uniform which was in such a disgusting state of muddiness that a dhobi could recall it after even one year, you persist in saying that it became so merely in making your way across a compound?'

'That compound was very, very neglected. It was a sea of mud only.'

'Indeed, Inspector? A sea of mud. What a very imaginative expression. Do you by any chance write poetry?'

'No, sir.'

'No? I am surprised. With your gift of invention you could make a great success of it. A greater success than you have had as a police officer, possibly.'

Out of the corner of his eye Ghote saw S. M. Motabhoy, not for the first time, direct a pointed look at Mrs Ahmed, as much as to say *Why are you not up on your feet protesting?*

'I mean,' R.K. continued, 'do you really intend to tell us, Inspector, that after less than one night's rain this compound had become – What were the words you chose? Ah, yes, a sea of mud?'

'The compound had been for some time very neglected.'

'So you are an expert in the management of a house, besides being one of our most cherished policeman poets?'

'I am not a poet, sir.'

'Nor any sort of expert in the management of a large compound?'

'Not an expert, sir. But I was able to observe that compound for a period of several weeks. The first time I was seeing it even a large bandicoot was running from that place.'

'Inspector, you excel yourself. A bandicoot? A large bandicoot? Whatever will that imagination of yours produce next?'

Ghote did not see fit to answer.

'Inspector, I represent the Presiding Officer at this Inquiry. I have asked you a question. Are you declining to reply?'

'No, sir.'

'No? Then be so good as to let us hear what answer you have.'

'To the question *What will my imagination produce next?*'

But at the Board table S. M. Motabhoy gave a short cough.

'I do not think, Mr Sankar, we shall be helped by that particular answer from Inspector Ghote.'

'As you please, sir. Then perhaps the inspector will deign to answer this: did you or did you not, Inspector Ghote, on the night of June the 24th or 25th last year assist A.D.I.G. Kelkar to dispose illegally of the body of one Sergeant Desai? Now, do not be in a hurry to favour us with more of your hot denials. Remember that we are here to elicit the truth. So, did you assist A.D.I.G. Kelkar on that night. Yes or no?'

Inspector Ghote drew in a calm breath.

'I did not in any way assist the said A.D.I.G. Kelkar,' he replied.

20

Ghote's denial, calmly delivered, brought to an end the day's proceedings. R. K. Sankar flung himself back in his heavy chair as much as to say *If you can believe that you will believe there are flowers in the sky*. But S. M. Motabhoy, plump behind his moon spectacles, after announcing that next day the sole business would be the Defendant's Statement added 'Not that, gentlemen, after the denial we have just listened to we need perhaps hear more from Inspector Ghote, though procedure under the Police Act must of course be rigidly adhered to.'

Ghote fought down a glint of hope then. He had, too, presence of mind enough to thank Mrs Ahmed for having stayed there, ostensibly his defender, before he set off for home.

But he did not get out of the building without experiencing a brief but unsettling incident. He was peering out at the rain, still from time to time wind-whipped to fury, and wondering whether to leave his scooter and endure the long wait for a bus and subsequent buffeting crowdedness when he came aware that someone was standing close behind him.

He turned, a little perturbed by the person's proximity.

And found himself face to face with the taut cheeks and glittering eyes of Inspector Pimputkar.

He would have preferred to say nothing to him. But standing as they were within a few inches of each other, he felt he could not simply move away without speaking.

'Terrible rains, Inspector,' he tried.

'No worse than when you set off for the lake at Vigatpore surely?' Pimputkar answered.

Ghote was shocked.

He was not even certain whether it was allowable for people on opposite sides in an Inquiry to discuss the case, though he felt that it was wrong. But for Pimputkar simply to take it that what he himself had sworn had not happened had in fact taken place, and that they both knew it, was too much. Far, far too much.

'Inspector, I do not know what you are meaning,' he said.

Pimputkar smiled, a little tight smile.

'Oh, come, Inspector, what is the old saying? "Speak the truth you are not in court."'

Ghote felt a red jet of rage leap up in him.

'How dare you make such insinuation,' he shouted. 'I am telling and telling the truth and it is you who is lying and lying. With your evidence from a known thief only, and your depending and relying on the spite and resentment of a fellow like Shivram Patel.'

Again Pimputkar smiled and a sharp look of malice came into his eyes.

'But true evidence I was producing, Inspector, except only two-three details, isn't it? It will be enough to finish you tomorrow.'

'No,' Ghote shot back. 'No, it will not. And you will not, Pimputkar, try as you may. You were not there to hear what S. M. Motabhoy was saying just only now. He was saying we do not need to hear more from Inspector Ghote after the so calm denial we were just listening to, except that full procedures must be adhered to. That is what he was saying.'

And he had the satisfaction of seeing Pimputkar look thoroughly disconcerted.

Pumped high with confidence after the exchange, he strode off through the blinding rain, seized his scooter, started it with a single fine banging kick and roared out into the street with something of the panache of a film hero going to save the heroine from the villain and his full band of goondas.

Nor did he, rather to his own surprise when the burst of rosy confidence had lost its charge, come a cropper on the journey. He had begun to expect fate was bound at least to land him and his machine in some foot-deep puddle, even if he did not skid into the path of an oncoming vehicle. But, except for a delay of a few minutes where a blown down tree had crushed three or four roadside stalls and ended up partly blocking the traffic, no upset occurred. He watched for a little the dozen or so men already busy sawing up this wondrous gift with as many more old crones and scrambling urchins snatching off twigs for firewood, and then managed to wheel his machine round and resume his journey.

The check did, however, give him time finally to sober up and when he reached home he let no hint escape him of the hope he now nurtured. He even deliberately omitted re-counting his one or two small triumphs under R. K. Sankar's needling. When next day he had been properly cleared, if he was, when the Show Cause notice in front of S. M. Motabhoy had not needed to be filled in, then he could 'remember' those one or two moments and, husband to wife, boast a little.

He spent the evening pondering the Defendant's State-ment which he would have to make next day. Thinking of the ups and downs of the Inquiry so far, and especially re-membering those final, magical words *Not that, gentlemen, after the denial we have just listened to we need perhaps hear more from Inspector Ghote* – he had surely by-hearted them exactly – he came to the conclusion that his best course was not to attempt at all to counter the points that had been made against him. Instead he would simply state, as clearly and well as he could, that he had in no way assisted Tiger.

Even though he had. Even though he had.

So he took a sheet of scrap paper and a pencil and, not without a good many crossings-out and puttings-back, eventually composed a short and complete denial. He would have liked to have been able to step outside, find somewhere quiet and speak aloud the words he had arrived at. But the rain was still cascading down and the wind battering away, so he had to content himself with a retreat to the bathroom. There, standing barefoot on the chilly concrete floor, he went through a murmured recital. Three times.

But by the end of the evening he felt moderately happy with what he had done.

He would be calm and reasonable. If he could impress the Board, and above all S. M. Motabhoy, with the manner in which he made his denial, he would have done all that he could under the circumstances.

So it was not without an undercurrent of optimism next day that he presented himself, shoes and Sam Browne polished to a new pitch of shininess, uniform pressed to the last inch of crease, in the big room at the Old Secretariat. Even without Mrs Ahmed's knowledge of courtroom tactics he felt he could survive.

The lashing rain of the early night had died right away before he had left home, and as he stepped into the room he saw through the tall windows that the leaden mass of cloud which had hung over the city with only a single break since the day he had first secured Mrs Ahmed's services was slowly rolling apart. There were large patches of blue sky and, as he crossed to his hard chair for the last time, a great ray of sunshine poured out to illuminate the green heads of the tossing palms round the Maidan.

He could not help hoping it was a sign.

S. M. Motabhoy entered the room almost immediately,

with an air of being quietly pleased both with himself and life. He took his place in the middle of the Board table, glanced at his watch and looked round to make sure everybody was present. They were, even Mrs Ahmed, faithful to the last, hard at work going through a smeary pamphlet of some wronged person's protest. So, with a rounded cough of warning, S. M. Motabhoy announced that they should begin.

At once R. K. Sankar stood up.

'Yes, Mr Sankar?'

'Mr Presiding Officer, you have been good enough to say more than once during the course of the Inquiry that you did not think it a good thing to be bound too closely by the rules and procedures of other places.'

'Yes, indeed. Such regulations as have been specifically laid down for us we must, of course, adhere to with strict exactitude, but I do not feel we should have been bound by rules applicable elsewhere. I trust you are not going to complain of that?'

'By no means, Mr Presiding Officer. I would like, in fact, to avail myself of your most praiseworthy, if I may say so, disregard of the legal niceties that so often bedevil proceedings elsewhere.'

'Yes, Mr Sankar?' S. M. Motabhoy said, with the barest trace of impatience.

'Sir, I would like with your permission, to recall Inspector Pimputkar, who has some additional important evidence which I believe the Board should be in possession of before it comes to any decision.'

Ghote felt sweat spring up all over his body, on his chest, blotching in a moment the smartness of his uniform shirt, on his legs, making them seem instantly sore, and all over his face in terrible give-away shining thick beads.

What new evidence had Pimputkar got? What could it be? How could the fellow now, at the last moment, have discovered something that would prove all he had told the

Inquiry himself was a concoction of lies? Or would this evidence be false, like his bringing forward Shivram Patel, merely a malignant reaction to those final words of S. M. Motabhoy's which he himself had repeated to him? But would such a falsity nevertheless convince the Board till this moment, surely, ready to believe in his declared innocence?

S. M. Motabhoy had been, in his usual manner, giving quiet consideration to the request. Now he spoke.

'Yes, Mr Sankar, so long as you can assure us that this new evidence is likely to be of real assistance to us, by all means introduce it before we ask Inspector Ghote to make his Statement.'

Of course he would agree to R.K.'s request. It was nothing less than just.

'Thank you, sir,' R.K. replied. 'And if I might trespass on your indulgence in one further matter . . . I believe it would assist us all if I were first to introduce in evidence the Report which the late A.D.I.G. Kelkar made after his Inspection of Vigatpore Police Station.'

Again S. M. Motabhoy considered, though more briefly this time.

'Very well, Mr Sankar, if you think that would also materially assist.'

'I do, sir. I have the Report here. It is not an especially long document in itself. Much of the detail is confined to appendices, with which I need not bother you. So, if you would care, sir, to read the main portion to the Inquiry, as you did with the late Mr Kelkar's confession, that perhaps would be the most convenient way of proceeding.'

'Very good, Mr Sankar.'

The orderly took the document – it consisted, Ghote saw, of a good many sheets of closely typed paper held together with a tag at the corner – and handed it to S. M. Motabhoy.

'The main report is contained in Pages One to Four,' R.K. said.

'And that is what you wish the Board to hear?'

'It is.'

'Very well.'

S. M. Motabhoy gave a little cough and began to read in his sonorous, well-rounded tones. Ghote listened, quivering internally with anxiety.

What was it, what could it be, in Tiger's report on his Inspection that could somehow have a bearing on his own lies, those lies Tiger had taken such care in his suicide note to allow him to make? And what evidence was Pimputkar going to produce to back up whatever it was?

But, strive as he might, he could pick out no single thing that might seem to contain even the beginnings of a clue. What could there be in the various failings Tiger had so sharply seized on, mostly Inspector Khan's, some of his own, that could be a give-away point? The unkept-up Bad Character Roll? The missing page from Khan's Case Diary? That First Information Report which Desai had actually just taken in when Tiger had hurled the inkpot? The missing chair L whatever-it-was?

And why should there be anything, he thought. How could there be really? After all, when Tiger had written his Report there had been nothing that he would have wished more completely to conceal than those few appalling hours when the two of them had first carried the dead weight of Desai's body out into the rain-battered night, had then borrowed that bicycle, had gone afterwards in their strange procession – watched at some point, yes, by the thief Piraji, all unknowing though they had been – had reached the lakeside, had been through the terrible business of stripping that slippery body as if the fool had actually been going for a midnight swim under the first onslaught of the monsoon and the yet more grim business of pumping water into the inner cavities and had finally tipped their burden from that nearly sinking boat into the black water.

With a pang of sharp sadness he heard S. M. Motabhoy read out finally Tiger's assessment of his own running of the station. Tiger, keeping to the promise he had made to be strictly correct, had not ignored his faults. *I find Ghote to be lacking to a certain extent in good disciplinary qualities in failing to reprimand with sufficient force slackness wherever found and in failing to insist upon unflagging standards of dress, behaviour and duty.* But he had ended with clear words of praise. *He has brought the station up to a better level in the short time he has been its in-charge and is to be commended.*

Could it be that? Were Pimputkar and R.K. going to claim that Tiger, owing him a heavy debt, had given him a much inflated assessment? Surely not. Tiger had praised him, certainly but not overmuch. And, damn it, his time at Vigatpore had brought out all his capabilities to the front. He had done well. He had. And Tiger's report did no more than acknowledge as much, with at the same time mentioning such faults as he had. And even there it had perhaps been harsh. In those words about failing to reprimand with sufficient force. They meant, surely, not being as fierily fierce as Tiger himself would have been. Well, there were two ways of looking at that. Would old Nadkarni have been as sharply furious with one and all as Tiger if he had been sent in his day as in-charge at Vigatpore?

No. No, he would not have been, of course. He would have confronted each offender with his fault, have pointed it out to him, exactly, quietly. And, by the very steadiness he showed, he would have brought about reform. Why, he might even have got Desai to behave slightly more sensibly. Certainly, no amount of shouting, no display of fury, had done much in that way.

Perhaps if he himself, instead of trying to act as Tiger would have done and shouting at Desai when he had caught him sending Shinde out to buy that famous cigarette, had behaved in Nadkarni's way the fellow would not have made such a mess of delivering the F.I.R. book to Tiger. Perhaps the inkpot would never have got spilt, if the whole business had been conducted quietly yet forcefully. And then the inkpot would not have been hurled in rage and Desai at this moment would be alive and well and hopelessly foolish.

Yes, Tiger's anger had often enough achieved results, better results than he himself would have got, but it had had its other side, too. When Tiger had thrown that inkpot it had not been out of any cleansing rage. It had been out of uncontrolled, dangerous anger. Just that.

S. M. Motabhoy, his reading at an end, gave another of his warning coughs.

'Well,' he said, 'that seems to give Inspector Ghote a good chit on the whole. What, Mr Sankar, is the relevance of it, if you please?'

'Sir, I think that will become obvious when we hear from Inspector Pimputkar.'

'Very good. Let us have the inspector up.'

The orderly left the room.

Ghote sat there, all thought frozen. He had speculated and speculated but had no more idea now of what this was all about than when R.K. had produced his bombshell.

The minutes passed.

Then footsteps became audible outside. The orderly's heavy tread in his solid chappals, and a lighter, sharper tap-tap-tap of Inspector Pimputkar's shoes.

The door opened and they came in. Pimputkar, a small plastic documents wallet under his arm, the tiniest of smiles playing on his mouth, went straight to the witness table.

'With your permission, Mr Presiding Officer,' R.K. said.

'Certainly, Mr Sankar.'

R.K. took a long look round the room, his gaze coming at last to rest on Ghote himself. Outside, a tail of dark cloud came and went across the sun sending the room into momentary gloom.

'Inspector Pimputkar,' R.K. began at last, 'will you tell us how it comes about that you have evidence to produce at this late stage of the Inquiry?'

'Yes, sir. Certainly. The evidence I have thought it vital to put before the Inquiry is in the form of a First Information Report. This was made out more than a year ago, and it may be that I shall be blamed for failing to see its significance during my early investigations.'

'And how did that come about, Inspector?' R.K. said, giving to the question a strong touch of artificial censure.

'Sir, I am thinking that when the officers of the Board are examining the said F.I.R., which is the fourth and last carbon copy only, they will see that I may not be too much at fault in failing to spot out the one important thing in the same.'

'Perhaps, Inspector, it would assist us all if you were to produce this First Information Report? I take it you have it with you.'

'Yes, sir, I have. Here it is.'

Pimputkar unzipped the documents wallet he had carried in and drew out from it with great care the F.I.R. book which from the black ink-stain on it Ghote at once recognised as indeed the very one Desai had taken in to Tiger. But how could it cast light on what had happened in the office then? Had it got a minute trace of blood on it? No, it could not have. It had stayed on the desk all the while and Desai had bled within a foot or two of the door. And in any case how could blood or even ink on an F.I.R. be a clue to what had actually happened?

The sunlight that had been streaming in again through the windows faded abruptly as another cloud was blown across the sun's face.

This time Ghote was certain, however irrational he knew he was being, that here was an omen.

21

At the Board table S. M. Motabhoy's plumpish, pale face took on an expression of deep gravity as he read the First Information Report which Inspector Pimputkar had produced.

'Mr Sankar,' he said at last, 'kindly correct me if I am in error, but I see the significance of this F.I.R. as being that it is an account, I suppose probably the sole remaining one since it is a fourth copy, of a serious crime that took place shortly after Inspector Ghote became the in-charge at Vigatpore P.S. This appears to involve the same Shivram Patel who gave false evidence to this Inquiry. It concerns an attack by hired goondas on the chairman of the dairy co-operative, the setting up of which deprived Shivram Patel of a very considerable income. Am I correct in my assumption?'

'Yes, sir,' R.K. said. 'Will you care now to hear Inspector Pimputkar's further evidence?'

Ghote was mystified.

The F.I.R. appeared indeed to be the very one that Desai had taken in for Tiger, with his own note attached to it. But they had got its date wrong. The incident, which it looked as if an attempt had been made to hush up, had taken place before he had arrived at Vigatpore. It must have done, or he would not have attached that note, now missing. So how had it come about that S. M. Motabhoy had stated, and R.K. had confirmed that the date was during his own time as in-charge? Was this some other, similar incident? But, no, there had been nothing, certainly nothing repeating the pattern of that attack, evidence of which it was quite possible that Inspector Khan, Shivram Patel's friend, might have tried to hide.

'Inspector,' R.K. was now asking Pimputkar, 'would you tell the Inquiry exactly how this important evidence came not to be put before us earlier?'

'Sir, I much regret but it was only last night, in filing away such documents I had possessed myself of in the course of my investigation and had finally decided were not relevant, that I was noticing the date on the F.I.R. in question. You will see it is altogether faint.'

'Yes,' said S. M. Motabhoy, peering at the F.I.R., 'I can confirm that the whole sheet is very faint. It is a matter I have had occasion to complain of many times. Officers making out First Information Reports will persist in using carbon sheets that are too old for the purpose.'

'Yes, sir,' said Pimputkar. 'But you will see that the date is such that it comes within Inspector Ghote's time as in-charge at Vigatpore.'

'Yes, yes. We are aware of that. Please proceed, Mr Sankar.'

'Certainly, Mr Presiding Officer.'

R.K. gave a little hem.

'Now, Inspector, will you tell us what you understood from this extremely faint fourth copy of an otherwise missing document, which I may say it was indeed perspicacious of you to recognise the significance of.'

'Yes, sir. As soon as I realised what was the date on this copy, which being in its book was not able to be destroyed, I saw that it indicated that Inspector Ghote had been guilty of a most serious suppression. I also considered that a senior officer of A.D.I.G. Kelkar's experience and determination could not have failed to spot out such.'

'Yes, Inspector, a plain deduction. And you went on from this to infer what?'

'Sir, that the late A.D.I.G. Kelkar must have withheld any mention concerning this lapse from his Report, and instead he awarded to Inspector Ghote top marks.'

'Yes, Inspector, we have heard A.D.I.G. Kelkar's words of praise for Inspector Ghote, remarkable for their fulsomeness in the light of what you have just told us. Now, what further inference were you able to make from all this?'

'Sir, I think it is one hundred percent clear that the late Mr Kelkar must have been under some considerable debt to Inspector Ghote to have done this, and, sir, taking that with all the other evidence I have been able to obtain, setting aside that not all of it proved cent per cent bonafide, it leads me to the inevitable conclusion that Inspector Ghote did indeed assist Mr Kelkar in every step of his illegal proceedings on the night of the 24th and the early hours of 25th of June last year.'

'Thank you, Inspector.'

Pimputkar turned to leave the witness table. S. M. Motabhoy coughed loudly.

'One moment, Inspector. I do not believe but that Inspector Ghote's counsel will wish to put questions to you about a matter that appears to tell so heavily against her client.'

He looked across at Mrs Ahmed.

Ghote turned and whispered furiously to her.

'Madam, it is lies, lies, lies. Madam, I am believing the fellow must have altered the date on that F.I.R. It was made out while Inspector Khan was in charge still at Vigatpore. It was. I am sure it was.'

Mrs Ahmed leant forward across her table until her face was only inches from Ghote's.

'Inspector,' she whispered back, 'do you still tell me what you told yesterday, that in fact you did assist Mr Kelkar?'

Ghote felt himself go pale.

But he had spoken the truth to her then, and would not now deny it.

'Yes, madam, I do.'

'Then I still cannot help you. You must do what you can for yourself when you come to make your Statement.'

She rose to her feet.

'Mr Presiding Officer,' she said. 'No questions.'

A frown appeared on S. M. Motabhoy's face.

'No questions, Mrs Ahmed?' he asked.

'No, sir.'

S. M. Motabhoy gave a long sigh. He looked all round the big room, from Mrs Ahmed to R. K. Sankar, from Inspector Pimputkar, standing behind the witness table with the faintest of smiles at the corners of his thin lips, to, at last, Ghote, rigid and facing the front now, on his hard chair.

'Very well,' he said at last. 'Then there remains nothing of our business but the Defendant's Statement, followed by the Board's decision, after which I shall, if necessary, insert whatever punishment I consider appropriate on the Show Cause notice and thus conclude our deliberations.'

He looked round again, letting his gaze rest for one extra moment on Mrs Ahmed, as if he hoped that even at this moment she would rise and request the right to question Inspector Pimputkar.

But Mrs Ahmed was as unmoving as a stone-carved goddess in her drab sari.

'Very well,' S. M. Motabhoy repeated. 'Inspector Ghote will you kindly rise and make your Defendant's Statement.'

Ghote pushed himself to his feet. He felt as if merely doing so was forcing his way under some downward-plunging weight and that he had energy left for nothing more.

'Yes, Inspector?'

He extracted from himself one final effort, and found issuing from dry mouth, dry lips, dry brain the words he had rehearsed and memorised the night before.

'Sir, gentlemen. I beg to state in my defence as follows: On the night of June the 24th last year when I was in-charge at Vigatpore Police Station and when also an Inspection was taking place under A.D.I.G. Kelkar, he was at about the hour of 11.30 pip emma still engaged in examining station records. I myself, knowing there was no further assistance I would be able to give him, placed myself off duty and returned per foot to the temporary quarter I had been allotted in the house of one Shivram Patel at a distance of approximately one kilometre from the said police station. I did not therefore witness any of the proceedings described by the late A.D.I.G. Kelkar in the note he was setting forth immediately prior to his suicide by shooting.'

He paused.

This, allowing for a lapse or two, was exactly what he had decided he would say the night before. He had not intended to add anything at all about the earlier accusations made against him. But that had been before Pimputkar had produced his new evidence with its faint carbon-copy date surely falsified.

'Sir, gentlemen,' he began again. 'I must also, however, deal with the newest evidence which Inspector Pimputkar . . .'

He trailed off, not knowing what to say or how to say it.

'Yes, Inspector?' S. M. Motabhoy prompted.

He looked up then, for the first time, directly at S. M. Motabhoy, his judge. And there poured out from him all the burning sense of injustice he had felt ever since Pimputkar had begun giving evidence, culminating in this last cunning move of his.

'It is lies, sir. Lies. That man wants nothing more than to pin me down in an illegal act. Yesterday, sir, I was telling him that you, sir, seemed to believe and accept my account, and so – So, sir, he was inventing this malicious falsehood. It is the F.I.R. you are having in front of you, sir: it was filled in and dated in Inspector Khan's time at Vigatpore. It was then also that the three top copies must have been disposed off, leaving only that faint one. And, sir, on that it would be easy-easy to alter the date by means of a superimposed sheet of carbon of the same blue colour. Sir, that is what must have been done, and, sir –'

'One moment, Inspector.'

S. M. Motabhoy spoke quietly but with authority.

'Inspector, what you are alleging is a most serious matter. But it is one that perhaps can be put to the test, possibly even here and now.'

He took up the F.I.R. book and held it in front of him, peering hard.

'Hm,' he said doubtfully.

He handed the ink-stained book to the officer sitting on his right. Again it was held up to the light, peered at and pondered over – and passed on.

Ghote, withdrawing his attention from the decision-making process in the half-expressed hope that by doing so he would somehow gain from the officer at the end of the row the verdict he needed, caught sight of Inspector Pimputkar standing at the witness table and concentrating such a beam of will on the pondering officer that it was almost visible.

Pimputkar wants me convicted above everything, he thought with a plunge of black dismay. It means everything to him to have me found guilty. And can his sheer willpower make that man there twisting and turning the F.I.R. book believe that there has been no forgery?

Then, damn it, he would try counter-willpower.

He turned back to the Board table and willed and hoped and willed.

And at last he seemed to have achieved at least a partial victory. The officer at the end of the row shook his head and handed the book back.

Tingling to bursting point with anxiety, Ghote watched as the book went along the line again to be inspected by the two officers on S. M. Motabhoy's left. They brought their heads together over it and murmured inaudibly to each other.

Was the one at the far end more optimistic than his colleague? For a moment or two Ghote believed so. But at last with gravely shaken heads they returned the book to S. M. Motabhoy.

He took it, held it up in front of himself once again and peered intently at the disputed page.

'Unfortunately the light –' he began to pronounce.

But then, at that exact moment, the cloud which had been obscuring the sun was swept away and a full flood of light came in through the tall windows.

'Yes,' said S. M. Motabhoy. 'Yes, I think I can indeed clearly distinguish that there are two dates written in the appropriate space here. Yes, two clearly, one on top of the other.'

He handed the F.I.R. to the officer beside him.

'Orderly,' he said, 'you will escort Inspector Pimputkar to the duty havildar and request the latter to hold him in his custody until we have time to take further action.'

'Yes, sir,' said the orderly.

As Pimputkar, glinting with fury, was led away, Ghote felt as if a true miracle had intervened to save him. No doubt it might have been possible to detect the alteration of the date in the laboratory, and perhaps S. M. Motabhoy would have consented to a postponement of the final part of the Inquiry until a proper examination had been made. But equally Pimputkar's forgery might never have come to light. It could not have consisted of more than two or three superimposed carbon strokes after all, and Pimputkar must have counted on the fact that, knowing he was indeed guilty, he would not succeed in challenging something that only underlined his guilt.

Because guilty he was. He had done what Pimputkar had worked out that he had done. If Pimputkar had lied flagrantly only really at the last gasp, he himself had lied and lied and lied again from start to finish.

As the door closed behind Pimputkar and the orderly, S. M. Motabhoy gave a little tap with the end of a pencil on the table in front of him.

'Inspector,' he said, looking directly at Ghote, 'I take it that you have now brought your Defendant's Statement to a close?'

Ghote was on the point of replying simply 'Yes, sir'. But what he actually said he could not, looking back afterwards, wholly account for.

For a moment he had hung poised. Then, casting everything aside, he had plunged. Words he had for so long debarred himself from saying now at last came tumbling and cascading from him.

'Sir, yes. Something more. Yes. Sir, I must inform the Inquiry that – that despite this last item of manufactured evidence, nevertheless – nevertheless everything Inspector Pimputkar has all along been alleging is one hundred and one percent true. Sir, I did on the night of June the 24th last year at Vigatpore assist the late A.D.I.G. Kelkar in everything he was doing. Sir, at that time I was proud to do it. Sir, Mr Kelkar killed Sergeant Desai by accident only, by the uttermost mischance. It was as he was stating in his dying confession, sir. Sergeant Desai had acted in a most stupid manner, and Mr Kelkar, sir, was most naturally highly enraged. He threw that inkpot, sir. I was there and I saw it happen. But it was a great misfortune that it was striking Desai at all and a yet more great that it was killing him. Sir, Mr Kelkar was an officer I was feeling the strongest admiration for. It was his way of driving himself and every officer and man under him by his fierce anger, sir. I admired – I was at the time admiring him for just only that. And so in consequence, sir, I became determined that, if at all possible, what had happened should appear not to have happened by one bit. For that reason I was acting as I did, sir. And only because A.D.I.G. Kelkar was not mentioning my share in our activities I had felt obliged to carry on in the manner he was, as it were, instructing me to.'

S. M. Motabhoy looked gravely across at him as he came to a stop.

Ghote was conscious that everybody in the whole room was staring at him, all the Board members, R.K. leaning now suddenly forward, even the shorthand writer and the orderly. And Mrs Ahmed. Mrs Ahmed, he felt almost sure, was looking at him with an expression of approval only just beneath the surface of her solid, time-lined features.

'And you now admit to all this?' S. M. Motabhoy asked. 'What you are now saying is the truth and the whole truth?'

'Yes, sir. It is. I was wishing, sir, to preserve an officer of A.D.I.G. Kelkar's drive and efficiency to continue his work as a senior police officer, to continue to use his anger whenever dereliction and slackness were found to punish and harass the same. For that reason I continued to present to one and all the false account he had bequeathed to me, hoping also that I myself could stay as a police officer and conduct myself as he had, believing fully at that time that this was altogether the best way a police officer should conduct himself.'

S. M. Motabhoy sat in silence for a few moments. Then he asked a last question, his words full and plangent in the expectant air.

'Believing at that time, Inspector? But is it that you still continue to believe this?'

'No, sir,' Ghote answered slowly. 'I am believing that Mr Kelkar's way is a very excellent way. But I see also now that there are other ways that first-class police work can be done.'

'Yes.'

Another silence fell in the big, still sunlit room.

S. M. Motabhoy looked to either side at his fellow Board members.

'Gentlemen,' he said, 'I do not think that after this change of heart on the part of Inspector Ghote we can do anything other than find him guilty as charged.'

One after another four heads nodded in agreement.

'Very well,' S. M. Motabhoy said, 'we find Inspector Ghote guilty.'

He sat looking down at the table in front of him, his face behind the moon-like spectacles showing for the first time some indication of tenseness, of a decision being painfully arrived at.

At last he gave a little puff of what might have been anger or suddenly gathered resolution, or sorrow that things were as they were.

'Inspector,' he said, 'I have considered, in attempting to decide what punishment I should recommend, not only the failures in duty with which you were charged and to which you have, very properly, at last admitted. But I have also taken into account the reasons you have given us for doing what you did. And I may say that they are reasons with which I sympathize. They do you credit. I do not hesitate to say it.'

He paused and drew in a long breath.

'Nevertheless,' he went on, 'I would be failing in my duty were I not to say that a penalty should be imposed, the most severe of penalties even. Your actions, Ghote, were in flagrant disregard of the rules of conduct laid down under police regulations. I cannot therefore suggest any punishment less than Dismissal.'

Ghote, at the word, sat plump down on to the chair behind him.

He had expected when he had found himself making his declaration that precise retribution, in so far as he had thought of consequences at all. He recognised that S. M. Motabhoy was being entirely just. But hearing the word said, *Dismissal*, it was borne in on him to the full what it meant. His life as he had lived it was now over. Finished.

Done with. He was no more a police officer. He was nothing. There was nothing more for him.

As if through some thick smeary glass he saw S. M. Motabhoy stand up, put on his cap, turn and, accompanied by his fellow Board members, make his way towards the door. He was aware, too, as vaguely, that all the others in the room were standing up, collecting together their belongings, preparing to leave.

The Inquiry was over. It had done its work. It had elicited the truth. It had left him, as he deserved to be left, ruined.

Then something he had seen without at all taking it in struck him. S. M. Motabhoy had forgotten a duty. He had omitted to fill in the Show Cause notice stating the nature of the proposed punishment, that legal obligation which had to be completed within the period of the Inquiry. If this were not done the Board's whole verdict would be completely nullified.

He almost jumped up, hurried over to the Board table, snatched up the stiff sheet, heavily printed in black, and ran after S. M. Motabhoy.

But he stopped himself, even before he had risen from his chair, confusion halting him in the course which all his training dictated.

Could it be . . . ? No, it was ridiculous. An officer of S. M. Motabhoy's seniority would never . . . And yet . . .

Suddenly in front of him there came the scurry of a quickly moving figure. It was the shorthand writer. The fellow had darted across to the table, seized the thick sheet and seeing that S. M. Motabhoy was actually on the point of leaving the room had set off at a run towards him.

Slowly Ghote got to his feet.

S. M. Motabhoy had just moved out into the corridor under the crooked photographs of past Inspectors-General. One of his fellow Board members caught him by the sleeve and said something to him. Was it an invitation of some sort?

Sir, my wife and I would be most pleased if one evening before your final retirement . . .

The shorthandwalla reached them. Ghote saw him thrust his head in between S. M. Motabhoy and the officer. He was saying something. Ghote made out an urgent *Sir, please, sir* . . .

S. M. Motabhoy could not but have heard. Yet he turned and, walking slowly and thoughtfully, went away along the corridor. The shorthandwalla stood there. In his hand, dangling, was the thick, blackly printed sheet.

Fat, creamy white clouds were lolloping across the deep blue sky. It was Nareli Purnima, Coconut Day, the fixed date on which the monsoon was held to be officially over. But there had, of course, been a shower that morning, and there might even be more to come.

At Chaupatti Beach, it seemed, half Bombay had congregated to immerse coconuts in the sea in traditional celebration. Inspector Ghote, about to leave to investigate a case at a university college some distance out of the city, had come with Protima and Ved to take his share in the festivities, Protima dressed in the new sari which Ghote, flush with his restored pay, had bought her.

They made their way slowly across the yielding sand through the packed crowd and the pressing vendors of ice cream and paper cones of tongue-tickling bhelpuri, of balloons and whistles and by the thousand of big green coconuts. Ghote stopped when he saw a really fat one and bought it for Ved.

Because that morning Protima had performed a long puja in front of her small statue of God Ganesha – Ghote had noticed that the fragrant smoking agarbati sticks she lit came from Ram Bhaskar Manufacturing Co. (Private) Ltd – they decided that this afternoon's rite should be the sole responsibility of young Ved, delightedly eager to take his share in the rites.

They reached at last the sea itself, still churned and muddy from the threshing monsoon waves but no longer a danger to bathers. Hundreds of them, indeed, were already in the water, carrying out their coconuts till they thought they had reached the right place to set them down. Some of the celebrating pilgrims, more anxious or more pious, had even hired boats and were well out to sea performing the rite.

At a word from Ghote, Ved solemnly set forth into the sandy water, chappals left in his parents' care and shorts rolled up as high as they would go on his long, slim legs.

Ghote watched him wade out, allowing the warm contentment he had felt at intervals ever since the Inquiry had ended to roll over him once more.

Twenty yards out, Ved lowered his head and reverently placed his plump coconut in the water. The outgoing tide took it, bobbing and bouncing, and wafted it away. For a little Ved stood and watched it.

Then, just as he was turning to come back in, half a dozen urchins, bare all but for ragged shorts, came in a whooping pack through the waves. Their leader seized the fat trophy and raised it high above his head in triumph.

It was a mistake.

Ved, mouth open in a yell of red rage, face dark with fury, shot towards him, knocked him flat into the water with a single butt of his head, recaptured the big shell and stood back grasping it and looking as if he was ready to brain any of the pack who thought of disputing its possession.

'Ved,' Protima called out in agitated remonstrance. 'Ved, come away. Come back.'

'No,' Ghote said, 'leave him. He is right to be in such a temper.'

Protima turned to him.

'Oh,' she said, 'it is right to be in such a rage, is it? Then, please, Mr Police Officer, why were you not also losing your temper and rebuking those boys? It is what you were telling me you were wishing to do when you saw some other urchins blocking a drain before the monsoon was setting in.'

It took Ghote a moment or two to frame his answer.

Then he smiled.

'No,' he said, 'it is best for me to keep my anger until a time when it will be truly needed.'

Out in the sea, Ved had waded further into the brown choppy wavelets. Reverently, once more he lowered his big green coconut. The strongly running tide took it swiftly away, ducking and dipping.

They watched in silence. Above them across the cheerful blue of the sky the puffy white clouds moved slowly on.

Ghote looked up at them.

'Yes, do you know?' he said. 'I am thinking monsoon is definitely finished now.'